MODERN HEROINES
Selected Short Stories

Lucy Maud Montgomery

MODERN HEROINES
Selected Short Stories

Lucy Maud Montgomery

Silvery Books

Contents

Lilian's Business Venture

Lilian Mitchell turned into the dry-goods store on Randall Street, just as Esther Miller and Ella Taylor came out. They responded coldly to her greeting and exchanged significant glances as they walked away.

Lilian's pale face crimsoned. She was a tall, slender girl of about seventeen, and dressed in mourning. These girls had been her close friends once. But that was before the Mitchells had lost their money. Since then Lilian had been cut by many of her old chums and she felt it keenly.

The clerks in the store were busy and Lilian sat down to wait her turn. Near to her two ladies were also waiting and chatting.

"Helen wants me to let her have a birthday party," Mrs. Saunders was saying wearily. "She has been promised it so long and I hate to disappoint the child, but our girl left last week, and I cannot possibly make all the cakes and things myself. I haven't the time or strength, so Helen must do without her party."

"Talking of girls," said Mrs. Reeves impatiently, "I am almost discouraged. It is so hard to get a good all-round one. The last one I had was so saucy I had to discharge her, and the one I have now cannot make decent bread. I never had good luck with bread myself either."

"That is Mrs. Porter's great grievance too. It is no light task to bake bread for all those boarders. Have you made your jelly yet?"

"No. Maria cannot make it, she says, and I detest messing with jelly. But I really must see to it soon."

At this point a saleswoman came up to Lilian, who made her small purchases and went out.

"There goes Lilian Mitchell," said Mrs. Reeves in an undertone. "She looks very pale. They say they are dreadfully poor since Henry Mitchell died. His affairs were in a bad condition, I am told."

"I am sorry for Mrs. Mitchell," responded Mrs. Saunders. "She is such a sweet woman. Lilian will have to do something, I suppose, and there is so little chance for a girl here."

Lilian, walking down the street, was wearily turning over in her mind the problems of her young existence. Her father had died the preceding spring. He had been a supposedly prosperous merchant; the Mitchells had always lived well, and Lilian was a petted and only child. Then came the shock of Henry Mitchell's sudden death and of financial ruin. His affairs were found to be hopelessly involved; when all the debts were paid there was left only the merest pittance—barely enough for house-rent—for Lilian and her mother to live upon. They had moved into a tiny cottage in an unfashionable locality, and during the summer Lilian had tried hard to think of something to do. Mrs. Mitchell was a delicate woman, and the burden of their situation fell on Lilian's young shoulders.

There seemed to be no place for her. She could not teach and had no particular talent in any line. There was no opening for her in Willington, which was a rather sleepy little place, and Lilian was almost in despair.

"There really doesn't seem to be any real place in the world for me, Mother," she said rather dolefully at the supper table. "I've no talent at all; it is dreadful to have been born without one. And yet I *must* do something, and do it soon."

And Lilian, after she had washed up the tea dishes, went upstairs and had a good cry.

But the darkest hour, so the proverb goes, is just before the dawn, and after Lilian had had her cry out and was sitting at her window in the dusk, watching a thin new moon shining over the trees down the street, her inspiration came to her. A minute later she whirled into the tiny sitting-room where her mother was sewing.

"Mother, our fortune is made! I have an idea!"

"Don't lose it, then," said Mrs. Mitchell with a smile. "What is it, my dear?"

Lilian sobered herself, sat down by her mother's side, and proceeded to recount the conversation she had heard in the store that afternoon.

"Now, Mother, this is where my brilliant idea comes in. You have often told me I am a born cook and I always have good luck. Now, tomorrow morning I shall go to Mrs. Saunders and offer to furnish all the good things for Helen's birthday party, and then I'll ask Mrs. Reeves and Mrs. Porter if I may make their bread for them. That will do for a beginning, I like cooking, you know, and I believe that in time I can work up a good business."

"It seems to be a good idea," said Mrs. Mitchell thoughtfully, "and I am willing that you should try. But have you thought it all out carefully? There will be many difficulties."

"I know. I don't expect smooth sailing right along, and perhaps I'll fail altogether; but somehow I don't believe I will."

"A great many of your old friends will think—"

"Oh, yes; I know *that* too, but I am not going to mind it, Mother. I don't think there is any disgrace in working for my living. I'm going to do my best and not care what people say."

Early next morning Lilian started out. She had carefully thought over the details of her small venture, considered ways and means, and decided on the most advisable course. She would not attempt too much, and she felt sure of success.

To secure competent servants was one of the problems of Willington people. At Drayton, a large neighbouring town, were several factories, and into these all the working girls from Willington had crowded, leaving very few who were willing to go out to service. Many of those who did were poor cooks, and Lilian shrewdly suspected that many a harassed housekeeper in the village would be glad to avail herself of the new enterprise.

Lilian was, as she had said of herself, "a born cook." This was her capital, and she meant to make the most of it. Mrs. Saunders listened to her businesslike details with surprise and delight.

"It is the very thing," she said. "Helen is so eager for that party, but I could not undertake it myself. Her birthday is Friday. Can you have everything ready by then?"

"Yes, I think so," said Lilian briskly, producing her notebook. "Please give me the list of what you want and I will do my best."

From Mrs. Saunders she went to Mrs. Reeves and found a customer as soon as she had told the reason of her call. "I'll furnish all the bread and rolls you need," she said, "and they will be good, too. Now, about your jelly. I can make good jelly, and I'll be very glad to make yours."

When she left, Lilian had an order for two dozen glasses of apple jelly, as well as a standing one for bread and rolls. Mrs. Porter was next visited and grasped eagerly at the opportunity.

"I know your bread will be good," she said, "and you may count on me as a regular customer."

Lilian thought she had enough on hand for a first attempt and went home satisfied. On her way she called at the grocery store with an order that surprised Mr. Hooper. When she told him of her plan he opened his eyes.

"I must tell my wife about that. She isn't strong and she doesn't like cooking."

After dinner Lilian went to work, enveloped in a big apron, and whipped eggs, stoned raisins, stirred, concocted, and baked until dark. When bedtime came she was so tired that she could hardly crawl upstairs; but she felt happy too, for the day had been a successful one.

And so also were the days and weeks and months that

followed. It was hard and constant work, but it brought its reward. Lilian had not promised more than she could perform, and her customers were satisfied. In a short time she found herself with a regular and growing business on her hands, for new customers were gradually added and always came to stay.

People who gave parties found it very convenient to follow Mrs. Saunders's example and order their supplies from Lilian. She had a very busy winter and, of course, it was not all plain sailing. She had many difficulties to contend with. Sometimes days came on which everything seemed to go wrong—when the stove smoked or the oven wouldn't heat properly, when cakes fell flat and bread was sour and pies behaved as only totally depraved pies can, when she burned her fingers and felt like giving up in despair.

Then, again, she found herself cut by several of her old acquaintances. But she was too sensible to worry much over this. The friends really worth having were still hers, her mother's face had lost its look of care, and her business was prospering. She was hopeful and wide awake, kept her wits about her and looked out for hints, and learned to laugh over her failures.

During the winter she and her mother had managed to do most of the work themselves, hiring little Mary Robinson next door on especially busy days, and now and then calling in the assistance of Jimmy Bowen and his hand sled to carry orders to customers. But when spring came Lilian prepared to open up her summer campaign on a much larger scale. Mary Robinson was hired for the season, and John Perkins was engaged to act as carrier with his express wagon. A summer kitchen was boarded in in the backyard, and a new range bought; Lilian began operations with a striking advertisement in the Willington *News* and an attractive circular sent around to all her patrons. Picnics and summer weddings were frequent. In bread and rolls her trade was brisk and constant. She also took orders for pickles, preserves, and jellies, and this became such a flourishing branch that a second assistant had to be hired.

It was a cardinal rule with Lilian never to send out any article that was not up to her standard. She bore the loss of her failures, and sometimes stayed up half of the night to fill an order on time. "Prompt and perfect" was her motto.

The long hot summer days were very trying, and sometimes she got very tired of it all. But when on the anniversary of her first venture she made up her accounts she was well pleased. To be sure, she had not made a fortune; but she had paid all their expenses, had a hundred dollars clear, and had laid the solid foundations of a profitable business.

"Mother," she said jubilantly, as she wiped a dab of flour from her nose and proceeded to concoct the icing for Blanche Remington's wedding cake, "don't you think my business venture has been a decided success?"

Mrs. Mitchell surveyed her busy daughter with a motherly smile. "Yes, I think it has," she said.

The Waking of Helen

Robert Reeves looked somewhat curiously at the girl who was waiting on him at his solitary breakfast. He had not seen her before, arriving at his summer boarding house only the preceding night.

It was a shabby farmhouse on the inland shore of a large bay that was noted for its tides, and had wonderful possibilities of light and shade for an impressionist. Reeves was an enthusiastic artist. It mattered little to him that the boarding accommodations were most primitive, the people uncultured and dull, the place itself utterly isolated, as long as he could revel in those transcendent sunsets and sunrises, those marvellous moonlights, those wonderful purple shores and sweeps of shimmering blue water.

The owner of the farm was Angus Fraser, and he and his wife seemed to be a reserved, uncouth pair, with no apparent interest in life save to scratch a bare living out of their few stony acres. He had an impression that they were childless and was at a loss to place this girl who poured his tea and brought in his toast. She did not resemble either Fraser or his wife. She was certainly not beautiful, being very tall and rather awkward, and dressed in a particularly unbecoming dark print wrapper. Her luxuriant hair was thick and black, and was coiled in a heavy knot at the nape of her neck. Her features were delicate but irregular, and her skin was very brown. Her eyes attracted Reeves's notice especially; they were large and dark and full of a half-unconscious, wistful longing, as if a prisoned soul behind them were vainly trying to reveal itself.

Reeves could find out nothing of her from herself, for

she responded to his tentative questions about the place in the briefest fashion. Afterwards he interviewed Mrs. Fraser cautiously, and ascertained that the girl's name was Helen Fraser, and that she was Angus's niece.

"Her father and mother are dead and we've brought her up. Helen's a good girl in most ways—a little obstinate and sulky now and then—but generally she's steady enough, and as for work, there ain't a girl in Bay Beach can come up to her in house or field. Angus calculates she saves him a man's wages clear. No, I ain't got nothing to say against Helen."

Nevertheless, Reeves felt somehow that Mrs. Fraser did not like her husband's niece. He often heard her scolding or nagging Helen at her work, and noticed that the latter never answered back. But once, after Mrs. Angus's tongue had been especially bitter, he met the girl hurrying along the hall from the kitchen with her eyes full of tears. Reeves felt as if someone had struck him a blow. He went to Angus and his wife that afternoon. He wished to paint a shore picture, he said, and wanted a model. Would they allow Miss Fraser to pose for him? He would pay liberally for her time.

Angus and his wife had no objection. They would pocket the money, and Helen could be spared a spell every day as well as not. Reeves told Helen of his plan himself, meeting her in the evening as she was bringing the cows home from the low shore pastures beyond the marsh. He was surprised at the sudden illumination of her face. It almost transfigured her from a plain, sulky-looking girl into a beautiful woman.

But the glow passed quickly. She assented to his plan quietly, almost lifelessly. He walked home with her behind the cows and talked of the sunset and the mysterious beauty of the bay and the purple splendour of the distant coasts. She listened in silence. Only once, when he spoke of the distant murmur of the open sea, she lifted her head and looked at him.

"What does it say to you?" she asked.

"It speaks of eternity. And to you?"

"It calls me," she answered simply, "and then I want to go out and meet it—and it hurts me too. I can't tell how or why. Sometimes it makes me feel as if I were asleep and wanted to wake and didn't know how."

She turned and looked out over the bay. A dying gleam of sunset broke through a cloud and fell across her hair. For a moment she seemed the spirit of the shore personified—all its mystery, all its uncertainty, all its elusive charm.

She has possibilities, thought Reeves.

Next day he began his picture. At first he had thought of painting her as the incarnation of a sea spirit, but decided that her moods were too fitful. So he began to sketch her as "Waiting"—a woman looking out across the bay with a world of hopeless longing in her eyes. The subject suited her well, and the picture grew apace.

When he was tired of work he made her walk around the shore with him, or row up the head of the bay in her own boat. He tried to draw her out, at first with indifferent success. She seemed to be frightened of him. He talked to her of many things—the far outer world whose echoes never reached her, foreign lands where he had travelled, famous men and women whom he had met, music, art and books. When he spoke of books he touched the right chord. One of those transfiguring flashes he delighted to evoke now passed over her plain face.

"That is what I've always wanted," she said hungrily, "and I never get them. Aunt hates to see me reading. She says it is a waste of time. And I love it so. I read every scrap of paper I can get hold of, but I hardly ever see a book."

The next day Reeves took his Tennyson to the shore and began to read the *Idylls of the King* to her.

"It is beautiful," was her sole verbal comment, but her rapt eyes said everything.

After that he never went out with her without a book—now one of the poets, now some prose classic. He was surprised by her quick appreciation of and sympathy with the finest passages. Gradually, too, she forgot her shyness and began to talk. She knew nothing of his world, but her own world she knew and knew well. She was a mine of traditional history about the bay. She knew the rocky coast by heart, and every old legend that clung to it. They drifted into making excursions along the shore and explored its wildest retreats. The girl had an artist's eye for scenery and colour effect.

"You should have been an artist," Reeves told her one day when she had pointed out to him the exquisite loveliness of a shaft of light falling through a cleft in the rocks across a dark-green pool at their base.

"I would rather be a writer," she said slowly, "if I could only write something like those books you have read to me. What a glorious destiny it must be to have something to say that the whole world is listening for, and to be able to say it in words that will live forever! It must be the noblest human lot."

"Yet some of those men and women were neither good nor noble," said Reeves gently, "and many of them were unhappy."

Helen dismissed the subject as abruptly as she always did when the conversation touched too nearly on the sensitive edge of her soul dreams.

"Do you know where I am taking you today?" she said.

"No—where?"

"To what the people here call the Kelpy's Cave. I hate to go there. I believe there is something uncanny about it, but I think you will like to see it. It is a dark little cave in the curve of a small cove, and on each side the headlands of rock run far out. At low tide we can walk right around, but when the tide comes in it fills the Kelpy's Cave. If you were there and let the tide come past the points, you would be drowned unless you could swim, for the rocks are so steep and high it is impossible to climb them."

Reeves was interested.

"Was anyone ever caught by the tide?"

"Yes," returned Helen, with a shudder. "Once, long

ago, before I was born, a girl went around the shore to the cave and fell asleep there—and the tide came in and she was drowned. She was young and very pretty, and was to have been married the next week. I've been afraid of the place ever since."

The treacherous cave proved to be a picturesque and innocent-looking spot, with the beach of glittering sand before it and the high gloomy walls of rock on either hand.

"I must come here some day and sketch it," said Reeves enthusiastically, "and you must be the Kelpy, Helen, and sit in the cave with your hair wrapped about you and seaweed clinging to it."

"Do you think a kelpy would look like that?" said the girl dreamily. "I don't. I think it is a wild, wicked little sea imp, malicious and mocking and cruel, and it sits here and watches for victims."

"Well, never mind your sea kelpies," Reeves said, fishing out his Longfellow. "They are a tricky folk, if all tales be true, and it is supposed to be a very rash thing to talk about them in their own haunts. I want to read you 'The Building of the Ship.' You will like it, I'm sure."

When the tide turned they went home.

"We haven't seen the kelpy, after all," said Reeves.

"I think I shall see him some day," said Helen gravely. "I think he is waiting for me there in that gloomy cave of his, and some time or other he will get me."

Reeves smiled at the gloomy fancy, and Helen smiled back at him with one of her sudden radiances. The tide was creeping swiftly up over the white sands. The sun was low and the bay was swimming in a pale blue glory. They parted at Clam Point, Helen to go for the cows and Reeves to wander on up the shore. He thought of Helen at first, and the wonderful change that had come over her of late; then he began to think of another face—a marvellously lovely one with blue eyes as tender as the waters before him. Then Helen was forgotten.

The summer waned swiftly. One afternoon Reeves took a fancy to revisit the Kelpy's Cave. Helen could not go. It was harvest time, and she was needed in the field.

"Don't let the kelpy catch you," she said to him half seriously. "The tide will turn early this afternoon, and you are given to day-dreaming."

"I'll be careful," he promised laughingly, and he meant to be careful. But somehow when he reached the cave its unwholesome charm overcame him, and he sat down on the boulder at its mouth.

"An hour yet before tide time," he said. "Just enough time to read that article on impressionists in my review and then stroll home by the sandshore."

From reading he passed to day-dreaming, and day-dreaming drifted into sleep, with his head pillowed on the rocky walls of the cave.

How long he had slept he did not know, but he woke with a start of horror. He sprang to his feet, realizing his position instantly. The tide was in—far in past the headlands already. Above and beyond him towered the pitiless unscalable rocks. There was no way of escape.

Reeves was no coward, but life was sweet to him, and to die like that—like a drowned rat in a hole—to be able to do nothing but wait for that swift and sure oncoming death! He reeled against the damp rock wall, and for a moment sea and sky and prisoning headlands and white-lined tide whirled before his eyes.

Then his head grew clearer. He tried to think. How long had he? Not more than twenty minutes at the outside. Well, death was sure and he would meet it bravely. But to wait—to wait helplessly! He should go; mad with the horror of it before those endless minutes would have passed!

He took something from his pocket and bent his, head over it, pressing his lips to it repeatedly. And then, when he raised his face again, a dory was coming around the headland on his right, and Helen Fraser was in it.

Reeves was dizzy again with the shock of joy and thankfulness. He ran down over the little stretch of sand still uncovered by the tide and around to the rocks of the headlands against which the dory was already grating.

He sprang forward impulsively and caught the girl's cold hands in his as she dropped the oars and stood up.

"Helen, you have saved me! How can I ever thank you? I—"

He broke off abruptly, for she was looking up at him, breathlessly and voicelessly, with her whole soul in her eyes. He saw in them a revelation that amazed him; he dropped her hands and stepped back as if she had struck him in the face.

Helen did not notice the change in him. She clasped her hands together and her voice trembled.

"Oh, I was afraid I should be too late! When I came in from the field Aunt Hannah said you had not come back—and I knew it was tide time—and I felt somehow that it had caught you in the cave. I ran down over the marsh and took Joe Simmon's dory. If I had not got here in time—"

She broke off shiveringly. Reeves stepped into the dory and took up the oars.

"The kelpy would have been sure of its victim then," he said, trying to speak lightly. "It would have almost served me right for neglecting your warning. I was very careless. You must let me row back. I am afraid you have overtasked your strength trying to cheat the kelpy."

Reeves rowed homeward in an absolute silence. Helen did not speak and he could not. When they reached the dory anchorage he helped her out.

"I think I'll go out to the Point for a walk," he said. "I want to steady my nerves. You must go right home and rest. Don't be anxious—I won't take any more chances with sea kelpies."

Helen went away without a word, and Reeves walked slowly out to the Point. He was grieved beyond measure at the discovery he believed he had made. He had never dreamed of such a thing. He was not a vain man, and was utterly free from all tendency to flirtation. It had never occurred to him that the waking of the girl's deep nature might be attended with disastrous consequences. He had honestly meant to help her, and what had he done?

He felt very uncomfortable; he could not conscientiously blame himself, but he saw that he had acted foolishly. And of course he must go away at once. And he must also tell her something she ought to know. He wished he had told her long ago.

The following afternoon was a perfect one. Reeves was sketching on the sandshore when Helen came. She sat down on a camp stool a little to one side and did not speak. After a few moments Reeves pushed away his paraphernalia impatiently.

"I don't feel in a mood for work," he said. "It is too dreamy a day—one ought to do nothing to be in keeping. Besides, I'm getting lazy now that my vacation is nearly over. I must go in a few days."

He avoided looking at her, so he did not see the sudden pallor of her face.

"So soon?" she said in a voice expressive of no particular feeling.

"Yes. I ought not to have lingered so long. My world will be forgetting me and that will not do. It has been a very pleasant summer and I shall be sorry to leave Bay Beach."

"But you will come back next summer?" asked Helen quickly. "You said you would."

Reeves nerved himself for his very distasteful task.

"Perhaps," he said, with an attempt at carelessness, "but if I do so, I shall not come alone. Somebody who is very dear to me will come with me—as my wife. I have never told you about her, Helen, but you and I are such good friends that I do not mind doing so now. I am engaged to a very sweet girl, and we expect to be married next spring."

There was a brief silence. Reeves had been vaguely afraid of a scene and was immensely relieved to find his fear unrealized. Helen sat very still. He could not see her face. Did she care, after all? Was he mistaken?

When she spoke her voice was perfectly calm.

"Thank you, it is very kind of you to tell me about her. I suppose she is very beautiful."

"Yes, here is her picture. You can judge for yourself."

Helen took the portrait from his hand and looked at it steadily. It was a miniature painted on ivory, and the face looking out from it was certainly lovely.

"It is no wonder you love her," said the girl in a low tone as she handed it back. "It must be strange to be so beautiful as that."

Reeves picked up his Tennyson.

"Shall I read you something? What will you have?"

"Read 'Elaine,' please. I want to hear that once more."

Reeves felt a sudden dislike to her choice.

"Wouldn't you prefer something else?" he asked, hurriedly turning over the leaves. "'Elaine' is rather sad. Shan't I read 'Guinevere' instead?"

"No," said Helen in the same lifeless tone. "I have no sympathy for Guinevere. She suffered and her love was unlawful, but she was loved in return—she did not waste her love on someone who did not want or care for it. Elaine did, and her life went with it. Read me the story."

Reeves obeyed. When he had finished he held the book out to her.

"Helen, will you take this Tennyson from me in remembrance of our friendship and of the Kelpy's Cave? I shall never forget that I owe my life to you."

"Thank you."

She took the book and placed a little thread of crimson seaweed that had been caught in the sand between the pages of "Elaine." Then she rose.

"I must go back now. Aunt will need me. Thank you again for the book, Mr. Reeves, and for all your kindness to me."

Reeves was relieved when the interview was over. Her calmness had reassured him. She did not care very much, after all; it was only a passing fancy, and when he was gone she would soon forget him.

He went away a few days later, and Helen bade him an impassive good-bye. When the afternoon was far spent she stole away from the house to the shore, with her Tennyson in her hand, and took her way to the Kelpy's Cave.

The tide was just beginning to come in. She sat down on the big boulder where Reeves had fallen asleep. Beyond stretched the gleaming blue waters, mellowing into a hundred fairy shades horizonward.

The shadows of the rocks were around her. In front was the white line of the incoming tide; it had almost reached the headlands. A few minutes more and escape would be cut off—yet she did not move.

When the dark green water reached her, and the lapping wavelets swished up over the hem of her dress, she lifted her head and a sudden strange smile flashed over her face.

Perhaps the kelpy understood it.

The Romance of Aunt Beatrice

Margaret always maintains that it was a direct inspiration of Providence that took her across the street to see Aunt Beatrice that night. And Aunt Beatrice believes that it was too. But the truth of the matter is that Margaret was feeling very unhappy, and went over to talk to Aunt Beatrice as the only alternative to a fit of crying. Margaret's unhappiness has nothing further to do with this story, so it may be dismissed with the remark that it did not amount to much, in spite of Margaret's tragical attitude, and was dissipated at once and forever by the arrival of a certain missent letter the next day.

Aunt Beatrice was alone. Her brother and his wife had gone to the "at home" which Mrs. Cunningham was giving that night in honour of the Honourable John Reynolds, M.P. The children were upstairs in bed, and Aunt Beatrice was darning their stockings, a big basketful of which loomed up aggressively on the table beside her. Or, to speak more correctly, she had been darning them. Just when Margaret was sliding across the icy street Aunt Beatrice was bent forward in her chair, her hands over her face, while soft, shrinking little sobs shook her from head to foot.

When Margaret's imperative knock came at the front door, Aunt Beatrice started guiltily and wished earnestly that she had waited until she went to bed before crying, if cry she must. She knew Margaret's knock, and she did not want her gay young niece, of all people in the world, to suspect the fact or the cause of her tears.

"I hope she won't notice my eyes," she thought, as she

hastily plumped a big ugly dark-green shade, with an almond-eyed oriental leering from it, over the lamp, before going out to let Margaret in.

Margaret did not notice at first. She was too deeply absorbed in her own troubles to think that anyone else in the world could be miserable too. She curled up in the deep easy-chair by the fire, and clasped her hands behind her curly head with a sigh of physical comfort and mental unhappiness, while Aunt Beatrice, warily sitting with her back to the light, took up her work again.

"You didn't go to Mrs. Cunningham's 'at home,' Auntie," said Margaret lazily, feeling that she must make some conversation to justify her appearance. "You were invited, weren't you?"

Aunt Beatrice nodded. The hole she was darning in the knee of Willie Hayden's stocking must be done very carefully. Mrs. George Hayden was particular about such matters. Perhaps this was why Aunt Beatrice did not speak.

"Why didn't you go?" asked Margaret absently, wondering why there had been no letter for her that morning—and this was the third day too! Could Gilbert be ill? Or was he flirting with some other girl and forgetting her? Margaret swallowed a big lump in her throat, and resolved that she would go home next week— no, she wouldn't, either—if he was as hateful and fickle as that—what was Aunt Beatrice saying?

"Well, I'm—I'm not used to going to parties now, my dear. And the truth is I have no dress fit to wear. At least Bella said so, because the party was to be a very fashionable affair. She said my old grey silk wouldn't do at all. Of course she knows. She had to have a new dress for it, and, we couldn't both have that. George couldn't afford it these hard times. And, as Bella said, it would be very foolish of me to get an expensive dress that would be no use to me afterward. But it doesn't matter. And, of course, somebody had to stay with the children."

"Of course," assented Margaret dreamily. Mrs. Cunningham's "at home" was of no particular interest.

The guests were all middle-aged people whom the M.P. had known in his boyhood and Margaret, in her presumptuous youth, thought it would be a very prosy affair, although it had made quite a sensation in quiet little Murraybridge, where people still called an "at home" a party plain and simple.

"I saw Mr. Reynolds in church Sunday afternoon," she went on. "He is very fine-looking, I think. Did you ever meet him?"

"I used to know him very well long ago," answered Aunt Beatrice, bowing still lower over her work. "He used to live down in Wentworth, you know, and he visited his married sister here very often. He was only a boy at that time. Then—he went out to British Columbia and—and—we never heard much more about him."

"He's very rich and owns dozens of mines and railroads and things like that," said Margaret, "and he's a member of the Dominion Parliament, too. They say he's one of the foremost men in the House and came very near getting a portfolio in the new cabinet. I like men like that. They are so interesting. Wouldn't it be awfully nice and complimentary to have one of them in love with you? Is he married?"

"I—I don't know," said Aunt Beatrice faintly. "I have never heard that he was."

"There, you've run the needle into your finger," said Margaret sympathetically.

"It's of no consequence," said Aunt Beatrice hastily.

She wiped away the drop of blood and went on with her work. Margaret watched her dreamily. What lovely hair Aunt Beatrice had! It was so thick and glossy, with warm bronze tones where the lamp-light fell on it under that hideous weird old shade. But Aunt Beatrice wore it in such an unbecoming way. Margaret idly wondered if she would comb her hair straight back and prim when she was thirty-five. She thought it very probable if that letter did not come tomorrow.

From Aunt Beatrice's hair Margaret's eyes fell to Aunt Beatrice's face. She gave a little jump. Had Aunt Beatrice been crying? Margaret sat bolt upright.

"Aunt Beatrice, did you want to go to that party?" she demanded explosively. "Now tell me the truth."

"I did," said Aunt Beatrice weakly. Margaret's sudden attack fairly startled the truth out of her. "It is very silly of me, I know, but I did want to go. I didn't care about a new dress. I'd have been quite willing to wear my grey silk, and I could have fixed the sleeves. What difference would it have made? Nobody would ever have noticed me, but Bella thought it wouldn't do."

She paused long enough to give a little sob which she could not repress. Margaret made use of the opportunity to exclaim violently, "It's a shame!"

"I suppose you don't understand why I wanted to go to this particular party so much," went on Aunt Beatrice shyly. "I'll tell you why—if you won't laugh at me. I wanted to see John Reynolds—not to talk to him—oh, I dare say he wouldn't remember me—but just to see him. Long ago—fifteen years ago—we were engaged. And—and—I loved him so much then, Margaret."

"You poor dear!" said Margaret sympathetically. She reached over and patted her aunt's hand. She thought that this little bit of romance, long hidden and unsuspected, blossoming out under her eyes, was charming. In her interest she quite forgot her own pet grievance.

"Yes—and then we quarrelled. It was a dreadful quarrel and it was about such a trifle. We parted in anger and he went away. He never came back. It was all my fault. Well, it is all over long ago and everybody has forgotten. I—I don't mind it now. But I just wanted to see him once more and then come quietly away."

"Aunt Beatrice, you are going to that party yet," said Margaret decisively.

"Oh, it is impossible, my dear."

"No, it isn't. Nothing is impossible when I make up my mind. You must go. I'll drag you there by main force if it comes to that. Oh, I have such a jolly plan, Auntie. You know my black and yellow dinner dress—no, you don't either, for I've never worn it here. The folks at home all said it was too severe for me—and so it is. Nothing suits me but the fluffy, chuffy things with a tilt to them. Gil—er—I mean—well, yes, Gilbert always declared that dress made me look like a cross between an unwilling nun and a ballet girl, so I took a dislike to it. But it's as lovely as a dream. Oh, when you see it your eyes will stick out. You must wear it tonight. It's just your style, and I'm sure it will fit you, for our figures are so much alike."

"But it is too late."

"'Tisn't. It's not more than half an hour since Uncle George and Aunt Bella went. I'll have you ready in a twinkling."

"But the fire—and the children!"

"I'll stay here and look after both. I won't burn the house down, and if the twins wake up I'll give them—what is it you give them—soothing syrup? So go at once and get you ready, while I fly over for the dress. I'll fix your hair up when I get back."

Margaret was gone before Aunt Beatrice could speak again. Her niece's excitement seized hold of her too. She flung the stockings into the basket and the basket into the closet.

"I will go—and I won't do another bit of darning tonight. I hate it—I hate it—I hate it! Oh, how much good it does me to say it!"

When Margaret came flying up the stairs Aunt Beatrice was ready save for hair and dress. Margaret cast the gown on the bed, revealing all its beauty of jetted lace and soft yellow silk with a dextrous sweep of her arm. Aunt Beatrice gave a little cry of admiration.

"Isn't it lovely?" demanded Margaret. "And I've brought you my opera cape and my fascinator and my black satin slippers with the cunningest gold buckles, and some sweet pale yellow roses that Uncle Ned gave me yesterday. Oh, Aunt Beatrice! What magnificent arms and shoulders you have! They're like marble. Mine are so scrawny I'm just ashamed to have people know they belong to me."

Margaret's nimble fingers were keeping time with her

tongue. Aunt Beatrice's hair went up as if by magic into soft puffs and waves and twists, and a golden rose was dropped among the bronze masses. Then the lovely dress was put on and pinned and looped and pulled until it fell into its simple, classical lines around the tall, curving figure. Margaret stepped back and clapped her hands admiringly.

"Oh, Auntie, you're beautiful! Now I'll pop down for the cloak and fascinator. I left them hanging by the fire."

When Margaret had gone Aunt Beatrice caught up the lamp and tiptoed shamefacedly across the hall to the icy-cold spare room. In the long mirror she saw herself reflected from top to toe—or was it herself! Could it be— that gracious woman with the sweet eyes and flushed cheeks, with rounded arms gleaming through their black laces and the cluster of roses nestling against the warm white flesh of the shoulder?

"I do look nice," she said aloud, with a little curtsey to the radiant reflection. "It is all the dress, I know. I feel like a queen in it—no, like a girl again—and that's better."

Margaret went to Mrs. Cunningham's door with her.

"How I wish I could go in and see the sensation you'll make, Aunt Beatrice," she whispered.

"You dear, silly child! It's just the purple and fine linen," laughed Aunt Beatrice. But she did not altogether think so, and she rang the doorbell unquailingly. In the hall Mrs. Cunningham herself came beamingly to greet her.

"My dear Beatrice! I'm so glad. Bella said you could not come because you had a headache."

"My headache got quite better after they left, and so I thought I would get ready and come, even if it were rather late," said Beatrice glibly, wondering if Sapphira had ever worn a black-and-yellow dress, and if so, might not her historic falsehood be traced to its influence?

When they came downstairs together, Beatrice, statuesque and erect in her trailing draperies, and Mrs. Cunningham secretly wondering where on earth Beatrice

Hayden had got such a magnificent dress and what she had done to herself to make her look as she did—a man came through the hall. At the foot of the stairs they met. He put out his hand.

"Beatrice! It must be Beatrice! How little you have changed!"

Mrs. Cunningham was not particularly noted in Murraybridge for her tact, but she had a sudden visitation of the saving grace at that moment, and left the two alone.

Beatrice put her hand into the M.P.'s.

"I am glad to see you," she said simply, looking up at him.

She could not say that he had not changed, for there was little in this tall, broad-shouldered man of the world, with grey glints in his hair, to suggest the slim, boyish young lover whose image she had carried in her heart all the long years.

But the voice, though deeper and mellower, was the same, and the thin, clever mouth that went up at one corner and down at the other in a humorous twist; and one little curl of reddish hair fell over his forehead away from its orderly fellows, just as it used to when she had loved to poke her fingers through it; and, more than all, the deep-set grey eyes looking down into her blue ones were unchanged. Beatrice felt her heart beating to her fingertips.

"I thought you were not coming," he said. "I expected to meet you here and I was horribly disappointed. I thought the bitterness of that foolish old quarrel must be strong enough to sway you yet."

"Didn't Bella tell you I had a headache?" faltered Beatrice.

"Bella? Oh, your brother's wife! I wasn't talking to her. I've been sulking in corners ever since I concluded you were not coming. How beautiful you are, Beatrice! You'll let an old friend say that much, won't you?"

Beatrice laughed softly. She had forgotten for years that she was beautiful, but the sweet old knowledge had come back to her again. She could not help knowing that he spoke the simple truth, but she said mirthfully,

"You've learned to flatter since the old days, haven't you? Don't you remember you used to tell me I was too thin to be pretty? But I suppose a bit of blarney is a necessary ingredient in the composition of an M.P."

He was still holding her hand. With a glance of dissatisfaction at the open parlour door, he drew her away to the little room at the end of the hall, which Mrs. Cunningham, for reasons known only to herself, called her library.

"Come in here with me," he said masterfully. "I want to have a long talk with you before the other people get hold of you."

When Beatrice got home from the party ten minutes before her brother and his wife, Margaret was sitting Turk fashion in the big armchair, with her eyes very wide open and owlish.

"You dear girlie, were you asleep?" asked Aunt Beatrice indulgently.

Margaret nodded. "Yes, and I've let the fire go out. I hope you're not cold. I must run before Aunt Bella gets here, or she'll scold. Had a nice time?"

"Delightful. You were a dear to lend me this dress. It was so funny to see Bella staring at it."

When Margaret had put on her hat and jacket she went as far as the street door, and then tiptoed back to the sitting-room. Aunt Beatrice was leaning back in the armchair, with a drooping rose held softly against her lips, gazing dreamily into the dull red embers.

"Auntie," said Margaret contritely, "I can't go home without confessing, although I know it is a heinous offence to interrupt the kind of musing that goes with dying embers and faded roses in the small hours. But it would weigh on my conscience all night if I didn't. I was asleep, but I wakened up just before you came in and went to the window. I didn't mean to spy upon anyone—but that street was bright as day! And if you will let an M.P. kiss you on the doorstep in glaring moonlight, you must expect to be seen."

"I wouldn't have cared if there had been a dozen onlookers," said Aunt Beatrice frankly, "and I don't believe he would either."

Margaret threw up her hands. "Well, my conscience is clear, at least. And remember, Aunt Beatrice, I'm to be bridesmaid—I insist upon that. And, oh, won't you ask me to visit you when you go down to Ottawa next winter? I'm told it's such a jolly place when the House is in session. And you'll need somebody to help you entertain, you know. The wife of a cabinet minister has to do lots of that. But I forgot—he isn't a cabinet minister yet. But he will be, of course. Promise that you'll have me, Aunt Beatrice, promise quick. I hear Uncle George and Aunt Bella coming."

Aunt Beatrice promised. Margaret flew to the door.

"You'd better keep that dress," she called back softly, as she opened it.

The Unhappiness of Miss Farquhar

Frances Farquhar was a beauty and was sometimes called a society butterfly by people who didn't know very much about it. Her father was wealthy and her mother came of an extremely blue-blooded family. Frances had been out for three years, and was a social favourite. Consequently, it may be wondered why she was unhappy.

In plain English, Frances Farquhar had been jilted— just a commonplace, everyday jilting! She had been engaged to Paul Holcomb; he was a very handsome fellow, somewhat too evidently aware of the fact, and Frances was very deeply in love with him—or thought herself so, which at the time comes to pretty much the same thing. Everybody in her set knew of her engagement, and all her girl friends envied her, for Holcomb was a matrimonial catch.

Then the crash came. Nobody outside the family knew exactly what did happen, but everybody knew that the Holcomb-Farquhar match was off, and everybody had a different story to account for it.

The simple truth was that Holcomb was fickle and had fallen in love with another girl. There was nothing of the man about him, and it did not matter to his sublimely selfish caddishness whether he broke Frances Farquhar's heart or not. He got his freedom and he married Maud Carroll in six months' time.

The Farquhars, especially Ned, who was Frances's older brother and seldom concerned himself about her except when the family honour was involved, were furious at the whole affair. Mr. Farquhar stormed, and Ned swore, and Della lamented her vanished role of bridemaid. As for Mrs. Farquhar, she cried and said it would ruin Frances's future prospects.

The girl herself took no part in the family indignation meetings. But she believed that her heart was broken. Her love and her pride had suffered equally, and the effect seemed disastrous.

After a while the Farquhars calmed down and devoted themselves to the task of cheering Frances up. This they did not accomplish. She got through the rest of the season somehow and showed a proud front to the world, not even flinching when Holcomb himself crossed her path. To be sure, she was pale and thin, and had about as much animation as a mask, but the same might be said of a score of other girls who were not suspected of having broken hearts.

When the summer came Frances asserted herself. The Farquhars went to Green Harbour every summer. But this time Frances said she would not go, and stuck to it. The whole family took turns coaxing her and had nothing to show for their pains.

"I'm going up to Windy Meadows to stay with Aunt Eleanor while you are at the Harbour," she declared. "She has invited me often enough."

Ned whistled. "Jolly time you'll have of it, Sis. Windy Meadows is about as festive as a funeral. And Aunt Eleanor isn't lively, to put it in the mildest possible way."

"I don't care if she isn't. I want to get somewhere where people won't look at me and talk about—that," said Frances, looking ready to cry.

Ned went out and swore at Holcomb again, and then advised his mother to humour Frances. Accordingly, Frances went to Windy Meadows.

Windy Meadows was, as Ned had said, the reverse of lively. It was a pretty country place, with a sort of fag-end by way of a little fishing village, huddled on a wind-swept bit of beach, locally known as the "Cove." Aunt Eleanor was one of those delightful people, so few and far between in this world, who have perfectly mastered the art of minding their own business exclusively. She left Frances in peace.

She knew that her niece had had "some love trouble or other," and hadn't gotten over it rightly.

"It's always best to let those things take their course," said this philosophical lady to her "help" and confidant, Margaret Ann Peabody. "She'll get over it in time—though she doesn't think so now, bless you."

For the first fortnight Frances revelled in a luxury of unhindered sorrow. She could cry all night—and all day too, if she wished—without having to stop because people might notice that her eyes were red. She could mope in her room all she liked. And there were no men who demanded civility.

When the fortnight was over, Aunt Eleanor took crafty counsel with herself. The letting-alone policy was all very well, but it would not do to have the girl die on her hands. Frances was getting paler and thinner every day—and she was spoiling her eyelashes by crying.

"I wish," said Aunt Eleanor one morning at breakfast, while Frances pretended to eat, "that I could go and take Corona Sherwood out for a drive today. I promised her last week that I would, but I've never had time yet. And today is baking and churning day. It's a shame. Poor Corona!"

"Who is she?" asked Frances, trying to realize that there was actually someone in the world besides herself who was to be pitied.

"She is our minister's sister. She has been ill with rheumatic fever. She is better now, but doesn't seem to get strong very fast. She ought to go out more, but she isn't able to walk. I really must try and get around tomorrow. She keeps house for her brother at the manse. He isn't married, you know."

Frances didn't know, nor did she in the least degree care. But even the luxury of unlimited grief palls, and Frances was beginning to feel this vaguely. She offered to go and take Miss Sherwood out driving.

"I've never seen her," she said, "but I suppose that doesn't matter. I can drive Grey Tom in the phaeton, if you like."

It was just what Aunt Eleanor intended, and she saw Frances drive off that afternoon with a great deal of satisfaction.

"Give my love to Corona," she told her, "and say for me that she isn't to go messing about among those shore people until she's perfectly well. The manse is the fourth house after you turn the third corner."

Frances kept count of the corners and the houses and found the manse. Corona Sherwood herself came to the door. Frances had been expecting an elderly personage with spectacles and grey crimps; she was surprised to find that the minister's sister was a girl of about her own age and possessed of a distinct worldly prettiness. Corona was dark, with a different darkness from that of Frances, who had ivory outlines and blue-black hair, while Corona was dusky and piquant.

Her eyes brightened with delight when Frances told her errand.

"How good of you and Miss Eleanor! I am not strong enough to walk far yet—or do anything useful, in fact, and Elliott so seldom has time to take me out."

"Where shall we go?" asked Frances when they started. "I don't know much about this locality."

"Can we drive to the Cove first? I want to see poor little Jacky Hart. He has been so sick—"

"Aunt Eleanor positively forbade that," said Frances dubiously. "Will it be safe to disobey her?"

Corona laughed.

"Miss Eleanor blames my poor shore people for making me sick at first, but it was really not that at all. And I want to see Jacky Hart so much. He has been ill for some time with some disease of the spine and he is worse lately. I'm sure Miss Eleanor won't mind my calling just to see him."

Frances turned Grey Tom down the shore road that ran to the Cove and past it to silvery, wind-swept sands, rimming sea expanses crystal clear. Jacky Hart's home proved to be a tiny little place overflowing with children. Mrs. Hart was a pale, tired-looking woman with the patient, farseeing eyes so often found among the women who watch sea and shore every day and night of their lives for those who sometimes never return.

She spoke of Jacky with the apathy of hopelessness. The doctor said he would not last much longer. She told all her troubles unreservedly to Corona in her monotonous voice. Her "man" was drinking again and the mackerel catch was poor.

When Mrs. Hart asked Corona to go in and see Jacky, Frances went too. The sick boy, a child with a delicate, wasted face and large, bright eyes, lay in a tiny bedroom off the kitchen. The air was hot and heavy. Mrs. Hart stood at the foot of the bed with her tragic face.

"We have to set up nights with him now," she said. "It's awful hard on me and my man. The neighbours are kind enough and come sometimes, but most of them have enough to do. His medicine has to be given every half hour. I've been up for three nights running now. Jabez was off to the tavern for two. I'm just about played out."

She suddenly broke down and began to cry, or rather whimper, in a heart-broken way.

Corona looked troubled. "I wish I could come tonight, Mrs. Hart, but I'm afraid I'm really not strong enough yet."

"I don't know much about sickness," spoke up Frances firmly, "but if to sit by the child and give him his medicine regularly is all that is necessary, I am sure I can do that. I'll come and sit up with Jacky tonight if you care to have me."

Afterwards, when she and Corona were driving away, she wondered a good deal at herself. But Corona was so evidently pleased with her offer, and took it all so much as a matter of course, that Frances had not the courage to display her wonder. They had their drive through the great green bowl of the country valley, brimming over with sunshine, and afterwards Corona made Frances go home with her to tea.

Rev. Elliott Sherwood had got back from his pastoral visitations, and was training his sweet peas in the way they should go against the garden fence. He was in his shirt sleeves and wore a big straw hat, and seemed in nowise disconcerted thereby. Corona introduced him, and he took Grey Tom away and put him in the barn. Then he went back to his sweet peas. He had had his tea, he said, so that Frances did not see him again until she went home. She thought he was a very indifferent young man, and not half so nice as his sister.

But she went and sat up with Jacky Hart that night, getting to the Cove at dark, when the sea was a shimmer of fairy tints and the boats were coming in from the fishing grounds. Jacky greeted her with a wonderful smile, and later on she found herself watching alone by his bed. The tiny lamp on the table burned dim, and outside, on the rocks, there was loud laughing and talking until a late hour.

Afterwards a silence fell, through which the lap of the waves on the sands and the far-off moan of the Atlantic surges came sonorously. Jacky was restless and wakeful, but did not suffer, and liked to talk. Frances listened to him with a new-born power of sympathy, which she thought she must have caught from Corona. He told her all the tragedy of his short life, and how bad he felt, about Dad's taking to drink and Mammy's having to work so hard.

The pitiful little sentences made Frances's heart ache. The maternal instinct of the true woman awoke in her. She took a sudden liking to the child. He was a spiritual little creature, and his sufferings had made him old and wise. Once in the night he told Frances that he thought the angels must look like her.

"You are so sweet pretty," he said gravely. "I never saw anyone so pretty, not even Miss C'rona. You look like a picture I once saw on Mr. Sherwood's table when I was up at the manse one day 'fore I got so bad I couldn't walk. It was a woman with a li'l baby in her arms and a kind of rim round her head. I would like something most awful much."

"What is it, dear?" said Frances gently. "If I can get or do it for you, I will."

"You could," he said wistfully, "but maybe you won't want to. But I do wish you'd come here just once every day and sit here five minutes and let me look at you—just that. Will it be too much trouble?"

Frances stooped and kissed him. "I will come every day, Jacky," she said; and a look of ineffable content came over the thin little face. He put up his hand and touched her cheek.

"I knew you were good—as good as Miss C'rona, and she is an angel. I love you."

When morning came Frances went home. It was raining, and the sea was hidden in mist. As she walked along the wet road, Elliott Sherwood came splashing along in a little two-wheeled gig and picked her up. He wore a raincoat and a small cap, and did not look at all like a minister—or, at least, like Frances's conception of one.

Not that she knew much about ministers. Her own minister at home—that is to say, the minister of the fashionable uptown church which she attended—was a portly, dignified old man with silvery hair and gold-rimmed glasses, who preached scholarly, cultured sermons and was as far removed from Frances's personal life as a star in the Milky Way.

But a minister who wore rubber coats and little caps and drove about in a two-wheeled gig, very much mud-bespattered, and who talked about the shore people as if they were household intimates of his, was absolutely new to Frances.

She could not help seeing, however, that the crisp brown hair under the edges of the unclerical-looking cap curled around a remarkably well-shaped forehead, beneath which flashed out a pair of very fine dark-grey eyes; he had likewise a good mouth, which was resolute and looked as if it might be stubborn on occasion; and, although he was not exactly handsome, Frances decided that she liked his face.

He tucked the wet, slippery rubber apron of his conveyance about her and then proceeded to ask questions. Jacky Hart's case had to be reported on, and then Mr. Sherwood took out a notebook and looked over its entries intently.

"Do you want any more work of that sort to do?" he asked her abruptly.

Frances felt faintly amused. He talked to her as he might have done to Corona, and seemed utterly oblivious of the fact that her profile was classic and her eyes delicious. His indifference piqued Frances a little in spite of her murdered heart. Well, if there was anything she could do she might as well do it, she told him briefly, and he, with equal brevity, gave her directions for finding some old lady who lived on the Elm Creek road and to whom Corona had read tracts.

"Tracts are a mild dissipation of Aunt Clorinda's," he said. "She fairly revels in them. She is half blind and has missed Corona very much."

There were other matters also—a dozen or so of factory girls who needed to be looked after and a family of ragged children to be clothed. Frances, in some dismay, found herself pledged to help in all directions, and then ways and means had to be discussed. The long, wet road, sprinkled with houses, from whose windows people were peering to see "what girl the minister was driving," seemed very short. Frances did not know it, but Elliott Sherwood drove a full mile out of his way that morning to take her home, and risked being late for a very important appointment—from which it may be inferred that he was not quite so blind to the beautiful as he had seemed.

Frances went through the rain that afternoon and read tracts to Aunt Clorinda. She was so dreadfully tired that night that she forgot to cry, and slept well and soundly.

In the morning she went to church for the first time since coming to Windy Meadows. It did not seem civil not to go to hear a man preach when she had gone slumming with his sister and expected to assist him with his difficulties over factory girls. She was surprised at Elliott Sherwood's sermon, and mentally wondered why such a man had been allowed to remain for four years in a little country pulpit. Later on Aunt Eleanor told her it was for his health.

"He was not strong when he left college, so he came here. But he is as well as ever now, and I expect he will soon be gobbled up by some of your city churches. He preached in Castle Street church last winter, and I believe they were delighted with him."

This was all of a month later. During that time Frances thought that she must have been re-created, so far was her old self left behind. She seldom had an idle moment; when she had, she spent it with Corona. The two girls had become close friends, loving each other with the intensity of exceptional and somewhat exclusive natures.

Corona grew strong slowly, and could do little for her brother's people, but Frances was an excellent proxy, and Elliott Sherwood kept her employed. Incidentally, Frances had come to know the young minister, with his lofty ideals and earnest efforts, very well. He had got into a ridiculous habit of going to her—her, Frances Farquhar!—for advice in many perplexities.

Frances had nursed Jacky Hart and talked temperance to his father and read tracts to Aunt Clorinda and started a reading circle among the factory girls and fitted out all the little Jarboes with dresses and coaxed the shore children to go to school and patched up a feud between two 'longshore families and done a hundred other things of a similar nature.

Aunt Eleanor said nothing, as was her wise wont, but she talked it over with Margaret Ann Peabody, and agreed with that model domestic when she said: "Work'll keep folks out of trouble and help 'em out of it when they are in. Just as long as that girl brooded over her own worries and didn't think of anyone but herself she was miserable. But as soon as she found other folks were unhappy, too, and tried to help 'em out a bit, she helped herself most of all. She's getting fat and rosy, and it is plain to be seen that the minister thinks there isn't the like of her on this planet."

One night Frances told Corona all about Holcomb. Elliott Sherwood was away, and Frances had gone up to stay all night with Corona at the manse. They were sitting in the moonlit gloom of Corona's room, and Frances felt confidential. She had expected to feel badly and cry a little while she told it. But she did not, and before she was half through, it did not seem as if it were worth telling after all. Corona was deeply sympathetic. She did not say a great deal, but what she did say put Frances on better terms with herself.

"Oh, I shall get over it," the latter declared finally. "Once I thought I never would—but the truth is, I'm getting over it now. I'm very glad—but I'm horribly ashamed, too, to find myself so fickle."

"I don't think you are fickle, Frances," said Corona gravely, "because I don't think you ever really loved that man at all. You only imagined you did. And he was not worthy of you. You are so good, dear; those shore people just worship you. Elliott says you can do anything you like with them."

Frances laughed and said she was not at all good. Yet she was pleased. Later on, when she was brushing her hair before the mirror and smiling absently at her reflection, Corona said: "Frances, what is it like to be as pretty as you are?"

"Nonsense!" said Frances by way of answer.

"It is not nonsense at all. You must know you are very lovely, Frances. Elliott says you are the most beautiful girl he has ever seen."

For a girl who has told herself a dozen times that she would never care again for masculine admiration, Frances experienced a very odd thrill of delight on hearing that the minister of Windy Meadows thought her beautiful. She knew he admired her intellect and had immense respect for what he called her "genius for influencing people," but she had really believed all along that, if Elliott Sherwood had been asked, he could not have told whether she was a whit better looking than Kitty Martin of the Cove, who taught a class in Sunday school and had round rosy cheeks and a snub nose.

The summer went very quickly. One day Jacky Hart died—drifted out with the ebb tide, holding Frances's hand. She had loved the patient, sweet-souled little creature and missed him greatly.

When the time to go home came Frances felt dull. She hated to leave Windy Meadows and Corona and her dear shore people and Aunt Eleanor and—and—well, Margaret Ann Peabody.

Elliott Sherwood came up the night before she went away. When Margaret Ann showed him reverentially in, Frances was sitting in a halo of sunset light, and the pale, golden chrysanthemums in her hair shone like stars in the blue-black coils.

Elliott Sherwood had been absent from Windy Meadows for several days. There was a subdued jubilance in his manner.

"You think I have come to say good-bye, but I haven't," he told her. "I shall see you again very soon, I hope. I have just received a call to Castle Street church, and it is my intention to accept. So Corona and I will be in town this winter."

Frances tried to tell him how glad she was, but only stammered. Elliott Sherwood came close up to her as she stood by the window in the fading light, and said—

But on second thoughts I shall not record what he said—or what she said either. Some things should be left to the imagination.

The Promise of Lucy Ellen

Cecily Foster came down the sloping, fir-fringed road from the village at a leisurely pace. Usually she walked with a long, determined stride, but to-day the drowsy, mellowing influence of the Autumn afternoon was strong upon her and filled her with placid content. Without being actively conscious of it, she was satisfied with the existing circumstances of her life. It was half over now. The half of it yet to be lived stretched before her, tranquil, pleasant and uneventful, like the afternoon, filled with unhurried duties and calmly interesting days, Cecily liked the prospect.

When she came to her own lane she paused, folding her hands on the top of the whitewashed gate, while she basked for a moment in the warmth that seemed cupped in the little grassy hollow hedged about with young fir-trees.

Before her lay sere, brooding fields sloping down to a sandy shore, where long foamy ripples were lapping with a murmur that threaded the hushed air like a faint minor melody.

On the crest of the little hill to her right was her home—hers and Lucy Ellen's. The house was an old-fashioned, weather-gray one, low in the eaves, with gables and porches overgrown with vines that had turned to wine-reds and rich bronzes in the October frosts. On three sides it was closed in by tall old spruces, their outer sides bared and grim from long wrestling with the Atlantic winds, but their inner green and feathery. On the fourth side a trim white paling shut in the flower garden before the front door. Cecily could see the beds of purple and scarlet asters, making rich whorls of color under the parlor and sitting-room windows. Lucy Ellen's bed was gayer and larger than Cecily's. Lucy Ellen had always had better luck with flowers.

She could see old Boxer asleep on the front porch step and Lucy Ellen's white cat stretched out on the parlor window-sill. There was no other sign of life about the place. Cecily drew a long, leisurely breath of satisfaction.

"After tea I'll dig up those dahlia roots," she said aloud. "They'd ought to be up. My, how blue and soft that sea is! I never saw such a lovely day. I've been gone longer than I expected. I wonder if Lucy Ellen's been lonesome?"

When Cecily looked back from the misty ocean to the house, she was surprised to see a man coming with a jaunty step down the lane under the gnarled spruces. She looked at him perplexedly. He must be a stranger, for she was sure no man in Oriental walked like that.

"Some agent has been pestering Lucy Ellen, I suppose," she muttered vexedly.

The stranger came on with an airy briskness utterly foreign to Orientalites. Cecily opened the gate and went through. They met under the amber-tinted sugar maple in the heart of the hollow. As he passed, the man lifted his hat and bowed with an ingratiating smile.

He was about forty-five, well, although somewhat loudly dressed, and with an air of self-satisfied prosperity pervading his whole personality. He had a heavy gold watch chain and a large seal ring on the hand that lifted his hat. He was bald, with a high, Shaksperian forehead and a halo of sandy curls. His face was ruddy and weak, but good-natured: his eyes were large and blue, and he had a little straw-colored moustache, with a juvenile twist and curl in it.

Cecily did not recognize him, yet there was something vaguely familiar about him. She walked rapidly up to the house. In the sitting-room she found Lucy Ellen peering out between the muslin window curtains. When the latter turned there was an air of repressed excitement about her.

"Who was that man, Lucy Ellen?" Cecily asked.

To Cecily's amazement, Lucy Ellen blushed—a warm, Spring-like flood of color that rolled over her delicate little face like a miracle of rejuvenescence.

"Didn't you know him? That was Cromwell Biron," she simpered. Although Lucy Ellen was forty and, in most respects, sensible, she could not help simpering upon occasion.

"Cromwell Biron," repeated Cecily, in an emotionless voice. She took off her bonnet mechanically, brushed the dust from its ribbons and bows and went to put it carefully away in its white box in the spare bedroom. She felt as if she had had a severe shock, and she dared not ask anything more just then. Lucy Ellen's blush had frightened her. It seemed to open up dizzying possibilities of change.

"But she promised—she promised," said Cecily fiercely, under her breath.

While Cecily was changing her dress, Lucy Ellen was getting the tea ready in the little kitchen. Now and then she broke out into singing, but always checked herself guiltily. Cecily heard her and set her firm mouth a little firmer.

"If a man had jilted me twenty years ago, I wouldn't be so overwhelmingly glad to see him when he came back— especially if he had got fat and bald-headed," she added, her face involuntarily twitching into a smile. Cecily, in spite of her serious expression and intense way of looking at life, had an irrepressible sense of humor.

Tea that evening was not the pleasant meal it usually was. The two women were wont to talk animatedly to each other, and Cecily had many things to tell Lucy Ellen. She did not tell them. Neither did Lucy Ellen ask any questions, her ill-concealed excitement hanging around her like a festal garment.

Cecily's heart was on fire with alarm and jealousy. She smiled a little cruelly as she buttered and ate her toast.

"And so that was Cromwell Biron," she said with studied carelessness. "I thought there was something familiar about him. When did he come home?"

"He got to Oriental yesterday," fluttered back Lucy Ellen. "He's going to be home for two months. We—we had such an interesting talk this afternoon. He—he's as full of jokes as ever. I wished you'd been here."

This was a fib. Cecily knew it.

"I don't, then," she said contemptuously. "You know I never had much use for Cromwell Biron. I think he had a face of his own to come down here to see you uninvited, after the way he treated you."

Lucy Ellen blushed scorchingly and was miserably silent.

"He's changed terrible in his looks," went on Cecily relentlessly. "How bald he's got—and fat! To think of the spruce Cromwell Biron got to be bald and fat! To be sure, he still has the same sheepish expression. Will you pass me the currant jell, Lucy Ellen?"

"I don't think he's so very fat," she said resentfully, when Cecily had left the table. "And I don't care if he is."

Twenty years before this, Biron had jilted Lucy Ellen Foster. She was the prettiest girl in Oriental then, but the new school teacher over at the Crossways was prettier, with a dash of piquancy, which Lucy Ellen lacked, into the bargain. Cromwell and the school teacher had run away and been married, and Lucy Ellen was left to pick up the tattered shreds of her poor romance as best she could.

She never had another lover. She told herself that she would always be faithful to the one love of her life. This sounded romantic, and she found a certain comfort in it.

She had been brought up by her uncle and aunt. When they died she and her cousin, Cecily Foster, found themselves, except for each other, alone in the world.

Cecily loved Lucy Ellen as a sister. But she believed that Lucy Ellen would yet marry, and her heart sank at the prospect of being left without a soul to love and care for.

It was Lucy Ellen that had first proposed their mutual

promise, but Cecily had grasped at it eagerly. The two women, verging on decisive old maidenhood, solemnly promised each other that they would never marry, and would always live together. From that time Cecily's mind had been at ease. In her eyes a promise was a sacred thing.

The next evening at prayer-meeting Cromwell Biron received quite an ovation from old friends and neighbors. Cromwell had been a favorite in his boyhood. He had now the additional glamour of novelty and reputed wealth.

He was beaming and expansive. He went into the choir to help sing. Lucy Ellen sat beside him, and they sang from the same book. Two red spots burned on her thin cheeks, and she had a cluster of lavender chrysanthemums pinned on her jacket. She looked almost girlish, and Cromwell Biron gazed at her with sidelong admiration, while Cecily watched them both fiercely from her pew. She knew that Cromwell Biron had come home, wooing his old love.

"But he sha'n't get her," Cecily whispered into her hymnbook. Somehow it was a comfort to articulate the words, "She promised."

On the church steps Cromwell offered his arm to Lucy Ellen with a flourish. She took it shyly, and they started down the road in the crisp Autumn moonlight. For the first time in ten years Cecily walked home from prayer-meeting alone. She went up-stairs and flung herself on her bed, reckless for once, of her second best hat and gown.

Lucy Ellen did not venture to ask Cromwell in. She was too much in awe of Cecily for that. But she loitered with him at the gate until the grandfather's clock in the hall struck eleven. Then Cromwell went away, whistling gaily, with Lucy Ellen's chrysanthemum in his buttonhole, and Lucy Ellen went in and cried half the night. But Cecily did not cry. She lay savagely awake until morning.

"Cromwell Biron is courting you again," she said bluntly to Lucy Ellen at the breakfast table.

Lucy Ellen blushed nervously.

"Oh, nonsense, Cecily," she protested with a simper.

"It isn't nonsense," said Cecily calmly. "He is. There is no fool like an old fool, and Cromwell Biron never had much sense. The presumption of him!"

Lucy Ellen's hands trembled as she put her teacup down.

"He's not so very old," she said faintly, "and everybody but you likes him—and he's well-to-do. I don't see that there's any presumption."

"Maybe not—if you look at it so. You're very forgiving, Lucy Ellen. You've forgotten how he treated you once."

"No—o—o, I haven't," faltered Lucy Ellen.

"Anyway," said Cecily coldly, "you shouldn't encourage his attentions, Lucy Ellen; you know you couldn't marry him even if he asked you. You promised."

All the fitful color went out of Lucy Ellen's face. Under Cecily's pitiless eyes she wilted and drooped.

"I know," she said deprecatingly, "I haven't forgotten. You are talking nonsense, Cecily. I like to see Cromwell, and he likes to see me because I'm almost the only one of his old set that is left. He feels lonesome in Oriental now."

Lucy Ellen lifted her fawn-colored little head more erectly at the last of her protest. She had saved her self-respect.

In the month that followed Cromwell Biron pressed his suit persistently, unintimidated by Cecily's antagonism. October drifted into November and the chill, drear days came. To Cecily the whole outer world seemed the dismal reflex of her pain-bitten heart. Yet she constantly laughed at herself, too, and her laughter was real if bitter.

One evening she came home late from a neighbor's. Cromwell Biron passed her in the hollow under the bare boughs of the maple that were outlined against the silvery moonlit sky.

When Cecily went into the house, Lucy Ellen opened the parlor door. She was very pale, but her eyes burned in her face and her hands were clasped before her.

"I wish you'd come in here for a few minutes, Cecily," she said feverishly.

Cecily followed silently into the room.

"Cecily," she said faintly, "Cromwell was here to-night. He asked me to marry him. I told him to come to-morrow night for his answer."

She paused and looked imploringly at Cecily. Cecily did not speak. She stood tall and unrelenting by the table. The rigidity of her face and figure smote Lucy Ellen like a blow. She threw out her bleached little hands and spoke with a sudden passion utterly foreign to her.

"Cecily, I want to marry him. I—I—love him. I always have. I never thought of this when I promised. Oh, Cecily, you'll let me off my promise, won't you?"

"No," said Cecily. It was all she said. Lucy Ellen's hands fell to her sides, and the light went out of her face.

"You won't?" she said hopelessly.

Cecily went out. At the door she turned.

"When John Edwards asked me to marry him six years ago, I said no for your sake. To my mind a promise is a promise. But you were always weak and romantic, Lucy Ellen."

Lucy Ellen made no response. She stood limply on the hearth-rug like a faded blossom bitten by frost.

After Cromwell Biron had gone away the next evening, with all his brisk jauntiness shorn from him for the time, Lucy Ellen went up to Cecily's room. She stood for a moment in the narrow doorway, with the lamplight striking upward with a gruesome effect on her wan face.

"I've sent him away," she said lifelessly. "I've kept my promise, Cecily."

There was silence for a moment. Cecily did not know what to say. Suddenly Lucy Ellen burst out bitterly.

"I wish I was dead!"

Then she turned swiftly and ran across the hall to her own room. Cecily gave a little moan of pain. This was her reward for all the love she had lavished on Lucy Ellen.

"Anyway, it is all over," she said, looking dourly into the moonlit boughs of the firs; "Lucy Ellen'll get over it. When Cromwell is gone she'll forget all about him. I'm not going to fret. She promised, and she wanted the promise first."

During the next fortnight tragedy held grim sway in the little weather-gray house among the firs—a tragedy tempered with grim comedy for Cecily, who, amid all her agony, could not help being amused at Lucy Ellen's romantic way of sorrowing.

Lucy Ellen did her mornings' work listlessly and drooped through the afternoons. Cecily would have felt it as a relief if Lucy Ellen had upbraided her, but after her outburst on the night she sent Cromwell away, Lucy Ellen never uttered a word of reproach or complaint.

One evening Cecily made a neighborly call in the village. Cromwell Biron happened to be there and gallantly insisted upon seeing her home.

She understood from Cromwell's unaltered manner that Lucy Ellen had not told him why she had refused him. She felt a sudden admiration for her cousin.

When they reached the house Cromwell halted suddenly in the banner of light that streamed from the sitting-room window. They saw Lucy Ellen sitting alone before the fire, her arms folded on the table, and her head bowed on them. Her white cat sat unnoticed at the table beside her. Cecily gave a gasp of surrender.

"You'd better come in," she said, harshly. "Lucy Ellen looks lonesome."

Cromwell muttered sheepishly, "I'm afraid I wouldn't be company for her. Lucy Ellen doesn't like me much—"

"Oh, doesn't she!" said Cecily, bitterly. "She likes you better than she likes me for all I've—but it's no matter. It's been all my fault—she'll explain. Tell her I said she could. Come in, I say."

She caught the still reluctant Cromwell by the arm and fairly dragged him over the geranium beds and through the front door. She opened the sitting-room door and pushed him in. Lucy Ellen rose in amazement. Over Cromwell's bald head loomed Cecily's dark face, tragic and determined.

"Here's your beau, Lucy Ellen," she said, "and I give you back your promise."

She shut the door upon the sudden illumination of

Lucy Ellen's face and went up-stairs with the tears rolling down her cheeks.

"It's my turn to wish I was dead," she muttered. Then she laughed hysterically.

"That goose of a Cromwell! How queer he did look standing there, frightened to death of Lucy Ellen. Poor little Lucy Ellen! Well, I hope he'll be good to her."

A Correspondence and A Climax

At sunset Sidney hurried to her room to take off the soiled and faded cotton dress she had worn while milking. She had milked eight cows and pumped water for the milk-cans afterward in the fag-end of a hot summer day. She did that every night, but tonight she had hurried more than usual because she wanted to get her letter written before the early farm bedtime. She had been thinking it out while she milked the cows in the stuffy little pen behind the barn. This monthly letter was the only pleasure and stimulant in her life. Existence would have been, so Sidney thought, a dreary, unbearable blank without it. She cast aside her milking-dress with a thrill of distaste that tingled to her rosy fingertips. As she slipped into her blue-print afternoon dress her aunt called to her from below. Sidney ran out to the dark little entry and leaned over the stair railing. Below in the kitchen there was a hubbub of laughing, crying, quarrelling children, and a reek of bad tobacco smoke drifted up to the girl's disgusted nostrils.

Aunt Jane was standing at the foot of the stairs with a lamp in one hand and a year-old baby clinging to the other. She was a big shapeless woman with a round good-natured face—cheerful and vulgar as a sunflower was Aunt Jane at all times and occasions.

"I want to run over and see how Mrs. Brixby is this evening, Siddy, and you must take care of the baby till I get back."

Sidney sighed and went downstairs for the baby. It never would have occurred to her to protest or be petulant about it. She had all her aunt's sweetness of disposition, if she resembled her in nothing else. She had not grumbled because she had to rise at four that morning, get breakfast, milk the cows, bake bread, prepare seven children for school, get dinner, preserve twenty quarts of strawberries, get tea, and milk the cows again. All her days were alike as far as hard work and dullness went, but she accepted them cheerfully and uncomplainingly. But she did resent having to look after the baby when she wanted to write her letter.

She carried the baby to her room, spread a quilt on the floor for him to sit on, and gave him a box of empty spools to play with. Fortunately he was a phlegmatic infant, fond of staying in one place, and not given to roaming about in search of adventures; but Sidney knew she would have to keep an eye on him, and it would be distracting to literary effort.

She got out her box of paper and sat down by the little table at the window with a small kerosene lamp at her elbow. The room was small—a mere box above the kitchen which Sidney shared with two small cousins. Her bed and the cot where the little girls slept filled up almost all the available space. The furniture was poor, but everything was neat—it was the only neat room in the house, indeed, for tidiness was no besetting virtue of Aunt Jane's.

Opposite Sidney was a small muslined and befrilled toilet-table, above which hung an eight-by-six-inch mirror, in which Sidney saw herself reflected as she devoutly hoped other people did not see her. Just at that particular angle one eye appeared to be as large as an orange, while the other was the size of a pea, and the mouth zigzagged from ear to ear. Sidney hated that mirror as virulently as she could hate anything. It seemed to her to typify all that was unlovely in her life. The mirror of existence into which her fresh young soul had looked for twenty years gave back to her wistful gaze just such distortions of fair hopes and ideals.

Half of the little table by which she sat was piled high

with books—old books, evidently well read and well-bred books, classics of fiction and verse every one of them, and all bearing on the flyleaf the name of Sidney Richmond, thereby meaning not the girl at the table, but her college-bred young father who had died the day before she was born. Her mother had died the day after, and Sidney thereupon had come into the hands of good Aunt Jane, with those books for her dowry, since nothing else was left after the expenses of the double funeral had been paid.

One of the books had Sidney Richmond's name printed on the title-page instead of written on the flyleaf. It was a thick little volume of poems, published in his college days—musical, unsubstantial, pretty little poems, every one of which the girl Sidney loved and knew by heart.

Sidney dropped her pointed chin in her hands and looked dreamily out into the moonlit night, while she thought her letter out a little more fully before beginning to write. Her big brown eyes were full of wistfulness and romance; for Sidney was romantic, albeit a faithful and understanding acquaintance with her father's books had given to her romance refinement and reason, and the delicacy of her own nature had imparted to it a self-respecting bias.

Presently she began to write, with a flush of real excitement on her face. In the middle of things the baby choked on a small twist spool and Sidney had to catch him up by the heels and hold him head downward until the trouble was ejected. Then she had to soothe him, and finally write the rest of her letter holding him on one arm and protecting the epistle from the grabs of his sticky little fingers. It was certainly letter-writing under difficulties, but Sidney seemed to deal with them mechanically. Her soul and understanding were elsewhere.

Four years before, when Sidney was sixteen, still calling herself a schoolgirl by reason of the fact that she could be spared to attend school four months in the winter when work was slack, she had been much interested in the "Maple Leaf" department of the Montreal weekly her uncle took. It was a page given over to youthful Canadians and filled with their contributions in the way of letters, verses, and prize essays. Noms de plume were signed to these, badges were sent to those who joined the Maple Leaf Club, and a general delightful sense of mystery pervaded the department.

Often a letter concluded with a request to the club members to correspond with the writer. One such request went from Sidney under the pen-name of "Ellen Douglas." The girl was lonely in Plainfield; she had no companions or associates such as she cared for; the Maple Leaf Club represented all that her life held of outward interest, and she longed for something more.

Only one answer came to "Ellen Douglas," and that was forwarded to her by the long-suffering editor of "The Maple Leaf." It was from John Lincoln of the Bar N Ranch, Alberta. He wrote that, although his age debarred him from membership in the club (he was twenty, and the limit was eighteen), he read the letters of the department with much interest, and often had thought of answering some of the requests for correspondents. He never had done so, but "Ellen Douglas's" letter was so interesting that he had decided to write to her. Would she be kind enough to correspond with him? Life on the Bar N, ten miles from the outposts of civilization, was lonely. He was two years out from the east, and had not yet forgotten to be homesick at times.

Sidney liked the letter and answered it. Since then they had written to each other regularly. There was nothing sentimental, hinted at or implied, in the correspondence. Whatever the faults of Sidney's romantic visions were, they did not tend to precocious flirtation. The Plainfield boys, attracted by her beauty and repelled by her indifference and aloofness, could have told that. She never expected to meet John Lincoln, nor did she wish to do so. In the correspondence itself she found her pleasure.

John Lincoln wrote breezy accounts of ranch life and

adventures on the far western plains, so alien and remote from snug, humdrum Plainfield life that Sidney always had the sensation of crossing a gulf when she opened a letter from the Bar N. As for Sidney's own letter, this is the way it read as she wrote it:

"The Evergreens," Plainfield.

Dear Mr. Lincoln:

The very best letter I can write in the half-hour before the carriage will be at the door to take me to Mrs. Braddon's dance shall be yours tonight. I am sitting here in the library arrayed in my smartest, newest, whitest, silkiest gown, with a string of pearls which Uncle James gave me today about my throat—the dear, glistening, sheeny things! And I am looking forward to the "dances and delight" of the evening with keen anticipation.

You asked me in your last letter if I did not sometimes grow weary of my endless round of dances and dinners and social functions. No, no, never! I enjoy every one of them, every minute of them. I love life and its bloom and brilliancy; I love meeting new people; I love the ripple of music, the hum of laughter and conversation. Every morning when I awaken the new day seems to me to be a good fairy who will bring me some beautiful gift of joy.

The gift she gave me today was my sunset gallop on my grey mare Lady. The thrill of it is in my veins yet. I distanced the others who rode with me and led the homeward canter alone, rocking along a dark, gleaming road, shadowy with tall firs and pines, whose balsam made all the air resinous around me. Before me was a long valley filled with purple dusk, and beyond it meadows of sunset and great lakes of saffron and rose where a soul might lose itself in colour. On my right was the harbour, silvered over with a rising moon. Oh, it was all glorious—the clear air with its salt-sea tang, the aroma of the pines, the laughter of my friends behind me, the spring and rhythm of Lady's grey satin body beneath me! I wanted to ride on so forever, straight into the heart of the sunset.

Then home and to dinner. We have a houseful of guests at present—one of them an old statesman with a massive silver head, and eyes that have looked into people's thoughts so long that you have an uncanny feeling that they can see right through your soul and read motives you dare not avow even to yourself. I was terribly in awe of him at first, but when I got acquainted with him I found him charming. He is not above talking delightful nonsense even to a girl. I sat by him at dinner, and he talked to me—not nonsense, either, this time. He told me of his political contests and diplomatic battles; he was wise and witty and whimsical. I felt as if I were drinking some rare, stimulating mental wine. What a privilege it is to meet such men and take a peep through their wise eyes at the fascinating game of empire-building!

I met another clever man a few evenings ago. A lot of us went for a sail on the harbour. Mrs. Braddon's house party came too. We had three big white boats that skimmed down the moonlit channel like great white sea birds. There was another boat far across the harbour, and the people in it were singing. The music drifted over the water to us, so sad and sweet and beguiling that I could have cried for very pleasure. One of Mrs. Braddon's guests said to me:

"That is the soul of music with all its sense and earthliness refined away."

I hadn't thought about him before—I hadn't even caught his name in the general introduction. He was a tall, slight man, with a worn, sensitive face and iron-grey hair—a quiet man who hadn't laughed or talked. But he began to talk to me then, and I forgot all about the others. I never had listened to anybody in the least like him. He talked of books and music, of art and travel. He had been all over the world, and had seen everything everybody else had seen and everything they hadn't too, I think. I seemed to be looking into an enchanted mirror where all my own dreams and ideals were reflected back to me, but made, oh, so much more beautiful!

On my way home after the Braddon people had left us somebody asked me how I liked Paul Moore! The man I had been talking with was Paul Moore, the great novelist! I was almost glad I hadn't known it while he was talking to me—I should have been too awed and reverential to have really enjoyed his conversation. As it was, I had contradicted him twice, and he had laughed and liked it. But his books will always have a new meaning to me henceforth, through the insight he himself has given me.

It is such meetings as these that give life its sparkle for me. But much of its abiding sweetness comes from my friendship with Margaret Raleigh. You will be weary of my rhapsodies over her. But she is such a rare and wonderful woman; much older then I am, but so young in heart and soul and freshness of feeling! She is to me mother and sister and wise, clear-sighted friend. To her I go with all my perplexities and hopes and triumphs. She has sympathy and understanding for my every mood. I love life so much for giving me such a friendship!

This morning I wakened at dawn and stole away to the shore before anyone else was up. I had a delightful run-away. The long, low-lying meadows between "The Evergreens" and the shore were dewy and fresh in that first light, that was as fine and purely tinted as the heart of one of my white roses. On the beach the water was purring in little blue ripples, and, oh, the sunrise out there beyond the harbour! All the eastern Heaven was abloom with it. And there was a wind that came dancing and whistling up the channel to replace the beautiful silence with a music more beautiful still.

The rest of the folks were just coming downstairs when I got back to breakfast. They were all yawny, and some were grumpy, but I had washed my being in the sunrise and felt as blithesome as the day. Oh, life is so good to live!

Tomorrow Uncle James's new vessel, the *White Lady*,

is to be launched. We are going to make a festive occasion of it, and I am to christen her with a bottle of cobwebby old wine.

But I hear the carriage, and Aunt Jane is calling me. I had a great deal more to say—about your letter, your big "round-up" and your tribulations with your Chinese cook—but I've only time now to say goodbye. You wish me a lovely time at the dance and a full programme, don't you?

Yours sincerely,
Sidney Richmond.

Aunt Jane came home presently and carried away her sleeping baby. Sidney said her prayers, went to bed, and slept soundly and serenely.

She mailed her letter the next day, and a month later an answer came. Sidney read it as soon as she left the post office, and walked the rest of the way home as in a nightmare, staring straight ahead of her with wide-open, unseeing brown eyes.

John Lincoln's letter was short, but the pertinent paragraph of it burned itself into Sidney's brain. He wrote:

I am going east for a visit. It is six years since I was home, and it seems like three times six. I shall go by the C.P.R., which passes through Plainfield, and I mean to stop off for a day. You will let me call and see you, won't you? I shall have to take your permission for granted, as I shall be gone before a letter from you can reach the Bar N. I leave for the east in five days, and shall look forward to our meeting with all possible interest and pleasure.

Sidney did not sleep that night, but tossed restlessly about or cried in her pillow. She was so pallid and hollow-eyed the next morning that Aunt Jane noticed it, and asked her what the matter was.

"Nothing," said Sidney sharply. Sidney had never spoken sharply to her aunt before. The good woman shook her head. She was afraid the child was "taking something."

"Don't do much today, Siddy," she said kindly. "Just

lie around and take it easy till you get rested up. I'll fix you a dose of quinine."

Sidney refused to lie around and take it easy. She swallowed the quinine meekly enough, but she worked fiercely all day, hunting out superfluous tasks to do. That night she slept the sleep of exhaustion, but her dreams were unenviable and the awakening was terrible.

Any day, any hour, might bring John Lincoln to Plainfield. What should she do? Hide from him? Refuse to see him? But he would find out the truth just the same; she would lose his friendships and respect just as surely. Sidney trod the way of the transgressor, and found that its thorns pierced to bone and marrow. Everything had come to an end—nothing was left to her! In the untried recklessness of twenty untempered years she wished she could die before John Lincoln came to Plainfield. The eyes of youth could not see how she could possibly live afterward.

*   *   *

Some days later a young man stepped from the C.P.R. train at Plainfield station and found his way to the one small hotel the place boasted. After getting his supper he asked the proprietor if he could direct him to "The Evergreens."

Caleb Williams looked at his guest in bewilderment. "Never heerd o' such a place," he said.

"It is the name of Mr. Conway's estate—Mr. James Conway," explained John Lincoln.

"Oh, Jim Conway's place!" said Caleb. "Didn't know that was what he called it. Sartin I kin tell you whar' to find it. You see that road out thar'? Well, just follow it straight along for a mile and a half till you come to a blacksmith's forge. Jim Conway's house is just this side of it on the right—back from the road a smart piece and no other handy. You can't mistake it."

John Lincoln did not expect to mistake it, once he found it; he knew by heart what it appeared like from

Sidney's description: an old stately mansion of mellowed brick, covered with ivy and set back from the highway amid fine ancestral trees, with a pine-grove behind it, a river to the left, and a harbour beyond.

He strode along the road in the warm, ruddy sunshine of early evening. It was not a bad-looking road at all; the farmsteads sprinkled along it were for the most part snug and wholesome enough; yet somehow it was different from what he had expected it to be. And there was no harbour or glimpse of distant sea visible. Had the hotel-keeper made a mistake? Perhaps he had meant some other James Conway.

Presently he found himself before the blacksmith's forge. Beside it was a rickety, unpainted gate opening into a snake-fenced lane feathered here and there with scrubby little spruces. It ran down a bare hill, crossed a little ravine full of young white-stemmed birches, and up another bare hill to an equally bare crest where a farmhouse was perched—a farmhouse painted a stark, staring yellow and the ugliest thing in farmhouses that John Lincoln had ever seen, even among the log shacks of the west. He knew now that he had been misdirected, but as there seemed to be nobody about the forge he concluded that he had better go to the yellow house and inquire within. He passed down the lane and over the little rustic bridge that spanned the brook. Just beyond was another home-made gate of poles.

Lincoln opened it, or rather he had his hand on the hasp of twisted withes which secured it, when he was suddenly arrested by the apparition of a girl, who flashed around the curve of young birch beyond and stood before him with panting breath and quivering lips.

"I beg your pardon," said John Lincoln courteously, dropping the gate and lifting his hat. "I am looking for the house of Mr. James Conway—'The Evergreens.' Can you direct me to it?"

"That is Mr. James Conway's house," said the girl, with the tragic air and tone of one driven to desperation and an impatient gesture of her hand toward the yellow nightmare above them.

"I don't think he can be the one I mean," said Lincoln perplexedly. "The man I am thinking of has a niece, Miss Richmond."

"There is no other James Conway in Plainfield," said the girl. "This is his place—nobody calls it 'The Evergreens' but myself. I am Sidney Richmond."

For a moment they looked at each other across the gate, sheer amazement and bewilderment holding John Lincoln mute. Sidney, burning with shame, saw that this stranger was exceedingly good to look upon—tall, clean-limbed, broad-shouldered, with clear-cut bronzed features and a chin and eyes that would have done honour to any man. John Lincoln, among all his confused sensations, was aware that this slim, agitated young creature before him was the loveliest thing he ever had seen, so lithe was her figure, so glossy and dark and silken her bare, wind-ruffled hair, so big and brown and appealing her eyes, so delicately oval her flushed cheeks. He felt that she was frightened and in trouble, and he wanted to comfort and reassure her. But how could she be Sidney Richmond?

"I don't understand," he said perplexedly.

"Oh!" Sidney threw out her hands in a burst of passionate protest. "No, and you never will understand— I can't make you understand."

"I don't understand," said John Lincoln again. "Can you be Sidney Richmond—the Sidney Richmond who has written to me for four years?"

"I am."

"Then, those letters—"

"Were all lies," said Sidney bluntly and desperately. "There was nothing true in them—nothing at all. This is my home. We are poor. Everything I told you about it and my life was just imagination."

"Then why did you write them?" he asked blankly. "Why did you deceive me?"

"Oh, I didn't mean to deceive you! I never thought of such a thing. When you asked me to write to you I wanted to, but I didn't know what to write about to a stranger. I just couldn't write you about my life here, not because it was hard, but it was so ugly and empty. So I wrote instead of the life I wanted to live—the life I did live in imagination. And when once I had begun, I had to keep it up. I found it so fascinating, too! Those letters made that other life seem real to me. I never expected to meet you. These last four days since your letter came have been dreadful to me. Oh, please go away and forgive me if you can! I know I can never make you understand how it came about."

Sidney turned away and hid her burning face against the cool white bark of the birch tree behind her. It was worse than she had even thought it would be. He was so handsome, so manly, so earnest-eyed! Oh, what a friend to lose!

John Lincoln opened the gate and went up to her. There was a great tenderness in his face, mingled with a little kindly, friendly amusement.

"Please don't distress yourself so, Sidney," he said, unconsciously using her Christian name. "I think I do understand. I'm not such a dull fellow as you take me for. After all, those letters were true—or, rather, there was truth in them. You revealed yourself more faithfully in them than if you had written truly about your narrow outward life."

Sidney turned her flushed face and wet eyes slowly toward him, a little smile struggling out amid the clouds of woe. This young man was certainly good at understanding. "You—you'll forgive me then?" she stammered.

"Yes, if there is anything to forgive. And for my own part, I am glad you are not what I have always thought you were. If I had come here and found you what I expected, living in such a home as I expected, I never could have told you or even thought of telling you what you have come to mean to me in these lonely years during which your letters have been the things most eagerly looked forward to. I should have come this evening and spent an hour or so with you, and then have gone away on the train tomorrow morning, and that would have been all.

"But I find instead just a dreamy romantic little girl, much like my sisters at home, except that she is a great deal cleverer. And as a result I mean to stay a week at Plainfield and come to see you every day, if you will let me. And on my way back to the Bar N I mean to stop off at Plainfield again for another week, and then I shall tell you something more—something it would be a little too bold to say now, perhaps, although I could say it just as well and truly. All this if I may. May I, Sidney?"

He bent forward and looked earnestly into her face. Sidney felt a new, curious, inexplicable thrill at her heart. "Oh, yes.—I suppose so," she said shyly.

"Now, take me up to the house and introduce me to your Aunt Jane," said John Lincoln in satisfied tone.

The Dissipation of Miss Ponsonby

We hadn't been very long in Glenboro before we managed to get acquainted with Miss Ponsonby. It did not come about in the ordinary course of receiving and returning calls, for Miss Ponsonby never called on anybody; neither did we meet her at any of the Glenboro social functions, for Miss Ponsonby never went anywhere except to church, and very seldom there. Her father wouldn't let her. No, it simply happened because her window was right across the alleyway from ours. The Ponsonby house was next to us, on the right, and between us were only a fence, a hedge of box, and a sprawly acacia tree that shaded Miss Ponsonby's window, where she always sat sewing—patchwork, as I'm alive—when she wasn't working around the house. Patchwork seemed to be Miss Ponsonby's sole and only dissipation of any kind.

We guessed her age to be forty-five at least, but we found out afterward that we were mistaken. She was only thirty-five. She was tall and thin and pale, one of those drab-tinted persons who look as if they had never felt a rosy emotion in their lives. She had any amount of silky, fawn-coloured hair, always combed straight back from her face, and pinned in a big, tight bun just above her neck—the last style in the world for any woman with Miss Ponsonby's nose to adopt. But then I doubt if Miss Ponsonby had any idea what her nose was really like. I don't believe she ever looked at herself critically in a mirror in her life. Her features were rather nice, and her expression tamely sweet; her eyes were big, timid, china-blue orbs that looked as if she had been badly scared when she was little and had never got over it; she never wore anything but black, and, to crown all, her first name was Alicia.

Miss Ponsonby sat and sewed at her window for hours at a time, but she never looked our way, partly, I suppose, from habit induced by modesty, since the former occupants of our room had been two gay young bachelors, whose names Jerry and I found out all over our window-panes with a diamond.

Jerry and I sat a great deal at ours, laughing and talking, but Miss Ponsonby never lifted her head or eyes. Jerry couldn't stand it long; she declared it got on her nerves; besides, she felt sorry to see a fellow creature wasting so many precious moments of a fleeting lifetime at patchwork. So one afternoon she hailed Miss Ponsonby with a cheerful "hello," and Miss Ponsonby actually looked over and said "good afternoon," as prim as an eighteen-hundred-and-forty fashion plate.

Then Jerry, whose name is Geraldine only in the family Bible, talked to her about the weather. Jerry can talk interestingly about anything. In five minutes she had performed a miracle—she had made Miss Ponsonby laugh. In five minutes more she was leaning half out of the window showing Miss Ponsonby a new, white, fluffy, frivolous, chiffony waist of hers, and Miss Ponsonby was leaning halfway out of hers looking at it eagerly. At the end of a quarter of an hour they were exchanging confidences about their favourite books. Jerry was a confirmed Kiplingomaniac, but Miss Ponsonby adored Laura Jean Libbey. She said sorrowfully she supposed she ought not to read novels at all since her father disapproved. We found out later on that Mr. Ponsonby's way of expressing disapproval was to burn any he got hold of, and storm at his daughter about them like the confirmed old crank he was. Poor Miss Ponsonby had to keep her Laura Jeans locked up in her trunk, and it wasn't often she got a new one.

From that day dated our friendship with Miss Ponsonby, a curious friendship, only carried on from window to window. We never saw Miss Ponsonby anywhere else; we asked her to come over but she said her father didn't allow her to visit anybody. Miss Ponsonby was one of those meek women who are ruled by whomsoever happens to be nearest them, and woe be unto them if that nearest happen to be a tyrant. Her meekness fairly infuriated Jerry.

But we liked Miss Ponsonby and we pitied her. She confided to us that she was very lonely and that she wrote poetry. We never asked to see the poetry, although I think she would have liked to show it. But, as Jerry says, there are limits.

We told Miss Ponsonby all about our dances and picnics and beaus and pretty dresses; she was never tired of hearing of them; we smuggled new library novels— Jerry got our cook to buy them—and boxes of chocolates, from our window to hers; we sat there on moonlit nights and communed with her while other girls down the street were entertaining callers on their verandahs; we did everything we could for her except to call her Alicia, although she begged us to do so. But it never came easily to our tongues; we thought she must have been born and christened Miss Ponsonby; "Alicia" was something her mother could only have dreamed about her.

We thought we knew all about Miss Ponsonby's past; but even pale, drab, china-blue women can have their secrets and keep them. It was a full half year before we discovered Miss Ponsonby's.

* * *

In October, Stephen Shaw came home from the west to visit his father and mother after an absence of fifteen years. Jerry and I met him at a party at his brother-in-law's. We knew he was a bachelor of forty-five or so and had made heaps of money in the lumber business, so we expected to find him short and round and bald, with bulgy blue eyes and a double chin. On the contrary, he was a tall, handsome man with clear-cut features, laughing black eyes like a boy's, and iron-grey hair. That iron-grey hair nearly finished Jerry; she thinks there is nothing so distinguished and she had the escape of her life from falling in love with Stephen Shaw.

He was as gay as the youngest, danced splendidly, went everywhere, and took all the Glenboro girls about impartially. It was rumoured that he had come east to look for a wife but he didn't seem to be in any particular hurry to find her.

One evening he called on Jerry; that is to say, he did ask for both of us, but within ten minutes Jerry had him mewed up in the cosy corner to the exclusion of all the rest of the world. I felt that I was a huge crowd, so I obligingly decamped upstairs and sat down by my window to "muse," as Miss Ponsonby would have said.

It was a glorious moonlight night, with just a hint of October frost in the air—enough to give sparkle and tang. After a few moments I became aware that Miss Ponsonby was also "musing" at her window in the shadow of the acacia tree. In that dim light she looked quite pretty. It was suddenly borne in upon me for the first time that, when Miss Ponsonby was young, she must have been very pretty, with that delicate elusive fashion of beauty which fades so early if the life is not kept in it by love and tenderness. It seemed odd, somehow, to think of Miss Ponsonby as young and pretty. She seemed so essentially middle-aged and faded.

"Lovely night, Miss Ponsonby," I said brilliantly.

"A very beautiful night, dear Elizabeth," answered Miss Ponsonby in that tired little voice of hers that always seemed as drab-coloured as the rest of her.

"I'm mopy," I said frankly. "Jerry has concentrated herself on Stephen Shaw for the evening and I'm left on the fringe of things."

Miss Ponsonby didn't say anything for a few moments. When she spoke some strange and curious note had come into her voice, as if a chord, long unswept and silent, had been suddenly thrilled by a passing hand.

"Did I understand you to say that Geraldine was—entertaining Stephen Shaw?"

"Yes. He's home from the west and he's delightful," I replied. "All the Glenboro girls are quite crazy over him. Jerry and I are as bad as the rest. He isn't at all young but he's very fascinating."

"Stephen Shaw!" repeated Miss Ponsonby faintly. "So Stephen Shaw is home again!"

"Why, I suppose you would know him long ago," I said, remembering that Stephen Shaw's youth must have been contemporaneous with Miss Ponsonby's.

"Yes, I used to know him," said Miss Ponsonby very slowly.

She did not say anything more, which I thought a little odd, for she was generally full of mild curiosity about all strangers and sojourners in Glenboro. Presently she got up and went away from her window. Deserted even by Miss Ponsonby, I went grumpily to bed.

Then Mrs. George Hubbard gave a big dance. Jerry and I were pleasantly excited. The Hubbards were the smartest of the Glenboro smart set and their entertainments were always quite brilliant affairs for a small country village like ours. This party was professedly given in honour of Stephen Shaw, who was to leave for the west again in a week's time.

On the evening of the party Jerry and I went to our room to dress. And there, across at her window in the twilight, sat Miss Ponsonby, crying. I had never seen Miss Ponsonby cry before.

"What is the matter?" I called out softly and anxiously.

"Oh, nothing," sobbed Miss Ponsonby, "only—only—I'm invited to the party tonight—Susan Hubbard is my cousin, you know—and I would like so much to go."

"Then why don't you?" said Jerry briskly.

"My father won't let me," said Miss Ponsonby, swallowing a sob as if she were a little girl of ten years old. Jerry had to dodge behind the curtain to hide a smile.

"It's too bad," I said sympathetically, but wondering a little why Miss Ponsonby seemed so worked up about it. I knew she had sometimes been invited out before and had not been allowed to go, but she had never cared apparently.

"Well, what is to be done?" I whispered to Jerry.

"Take Miss Ponsonby to the party with us, of course," said Jerry, popping out from behind the curtain.

I didn't ask her if she expected to fly through the air with Miss Ponsonby, although short of that I couldn't see how the latter was to be got out of the house without her father knowing. The old gentleman had a den off the hall where he always sat in the evening and smoked fiercely, after having locked all the doors to keep the servants in. He was a delightful sort of person, that old Mr. Ponsonby.

Jerry poked her head as far as she could out of the window. "Miss Ponsonby, you are going to the dance," she said in a cautious undertone, "so don't cry any more or your eyes will be dreadfully red."

"It is impossible," said Miss Ponsonby resignedly.

"Nothing is impossible when I make up my mind," said Jerry firmly. "You must get dressed, climb down that acacia tree, and join us in our yard. It will be pitch dark in a few minutes and your father will never know."

I had a frantic vision of Miss Ponsonby scrambling down that acacia tree like an eloping damsel. But Jerry was in dead earnest, and really it was quite possible if Miss Ponsonby only thought so. I did not believe she would think so, but I was mistaken. Her thorough course in Libbey heroines and their marvellous escapades had quite prepared her to contemplate such an adventure calmly—in the abstract at least. But another obstacle presented itself.

"It's impossible," she said again, after her first flash hope. "I haven't a fit dress to wear—I've nothing at all but my black cashmere and it is three years old."

But the more hindrances in Jerry's way when she sets out to accomplish something the more determined and enthusiastic she becomes. I listened to her with amazement.

"I have a dress I'll lend you," she said resolutely. "And I'll go over and fix you up as soon as it's a little darker. Go now and bathe your eyes and just trust to me."

Miss Ponsonby's long habit of obedience to whatever she was told stood her in good stead now. She obeyed Jerry without another word. Jerry seized me by the waist and waltzed me around the room in an ecstasy.

"Jerry Elliott, how are you going to carry this thing through?" I demanded sternly.

"Easily enough," responded Jerry. "You know that black lace dress of mine—the one with the apricot slip. I've never worn it since I came to Glenboro, so nobody will know it's mine, and I never mean to wear it again for it's got too tight. It's a trifle old-fashioned, but that won't matter for Glenboro, and it will fit Miss Ponsonby all right. She's about my height and figure. I'm determined that poor soul shall have a dissipation for once in her life since she hankers for it. Come on now, Elizabeth. It will be a lark."

I caught Jerry's enthusiasm, and while she hunted out the box containing the black lace dress, I hastily gathered together some other odds and ends I thought might be useful—a black aigrette, a pair of black silk gloves, a spangled gauze fan, and a pair of slippers. They wouldn't have stood daylight, but they looked all right after night. As we left the room I caught up some pale pink roses on my table.

We pushed through a little gap in the privet hedge and found ourselves under the acacia tree with Miss Ponsonby peering anxiously at us from above. I wanted to shriek with laughter, the whole thing seemed so funny and unreal. Jerry, although she hasn't climbed trees since she was twelve, went up that acacia as nimbly as a pussy-cat, took the box and things from me, passed them to Miss Ponsonby, and got in at the window while I went back to my own room to dress, hoping old Mr. Ponsonby wouldn't be running out to ring the fire alarm.

In a very short time I heard Miss Ponsonby and Jerry at the opposite window, and I rushed to mine to see the sight. But Miss Ponsonby, with a red fascinator over her head and a big cape wrapped round her, slipped out of the window and down that blessed acacia tree as neatly and nimbly as if she had been accustomed to doing it for exercise every day of her life. There were possibilities in Miss Ponsonby. In two more minutes they were both safe in our room.

Then Jerry threw off Miss Ponsonby's wraps and stepped back. I know I stared until my eyes stuck out of my head. Was that Miss Ponsonby—that!

The black lace dress, with the pinkish sheen of its slip beneath, suited her slim shape to perfection and clung around her in lovely, filmy curves that made her look willowy and girlish. It was high-necked, just cut away slightly at the throat, and had great, loose, hanging frilly sleeves of lace. Jerry had shaken out her hair and piled it high on her head in satiny twists and loops, with a pompadour such as Miss Ponsonby could never have thought about. It suited her tremendously and seemed to alter the whole character of her face, giving verve and piquancy to her delicate little features. The excitement had flushed her cheeks into positive pinkness and her eyes were starry. The roses were pinned on her shoulder. Miss Ponsonby, as she stood there, was a pretty woman, with fifteen apparent birthdays the less.

"Oh, Alicia, you look just lovely!" I gasped. The name slipped out quite naturally. I never thought about it at all.

"My dear Elizabeth," she said, "it's like a dream of lost youth."

We got Jerry ready and then we started for the Hubbards', out by our back door and through our neighbour-on-the-left's lane to avoid all observation. Miss Ponsonby was breathless with terror. She was sure every footstep she heard behind her was her father's in pursuit.

She almost fainted on the spot when a belated man came tearing along the street. Jerry and I breathed a sigh of devout thanksgiving when we found ourselves safely in the Hubbard parlour.

We were early, but Stephen Shaw was there before us. He came up to us at once, and just then Miss Ponsonby turned around.

"Alicia!" he said.

"How do you do, Stephen?" she said tremulously.

And there he was looking down at her with an expression on his face that none of the Glenboro girls he had been calling on had ever seen. Jerry and I just simply melted away. We can see through grindstones when there are holes in them!

We went out and sat down on the stairs.

"There's a mystery here," said Jerry, "but Miss Ponsonby shall explain it to us before we let her climb up that acacia tree tonight. Now that I come to think of it, the first night he called he asked me about her. Wanted to know if her father were the same old blustering tyrant he always was, and if we knew her at all. I'm afraid I made a little mild fun of her, and he didn't say anything more. Well, I'm awfully glad now that I didn't fall in love with him. I could have, but I wouldn't."

Miss Ponsonby's appearance at the Hubbards' party was the biggest sensation Glenboro had had for years. And in her way, she was a positive belle. She didn't dance, but all the middle-aged men, widowers, wedded, and bachelors, who had known her in her girlhood crowded around her, and she laughed and chatted as I hadn't even imagined Miss Ponsonby could laugh and chat. Jerry and I revelled in her triumph, for did we not feel that it was due to us? At last Miss Ponsonby disappeared; shortly after Jerry and I blundered into the library to fix some obstreperous hairpins, and there we found her and Stephen Shaw in the cosy corner.

There were no explanations on the road home, for Miss Ponsonby walked behind us with Stephen Shaw in the pale, late-risen October moonshine. But when we had sneaked through the neighbour-to-the-left's lane and reached our side verandah we waited for her, and as soon as Stephen Shaw had gone we laid violent hands on Miss Ponsonby and made her 'fess up there on the dark, chilly verandah, at one o'clock in the morning.

"Miss Ponsonby," said Jerry, "before we assist you in returning to those ancestral halls of yours you've simply got to tell us what all this means."

Miss Ponsonby gave a little, shy, nervous laugh.

"Stephen Shaw and I were engaged to be married long ago," she said simply. "But Father disapproved. Stephen was poor then. And so—and so—I sent him away. What else could I do?"—for Jerry had snorted—"Father had to be obeyed. But it broke my heart. Stephen went away— he was very angry—and I have never seen him since. When Susan Hubbard invited me to the party I felt as if I must go—I must see Stephen once more. I never thought for a minute that he remembered me—or cared still...."

"But he does?" said Jerry breathlessly. Jerry never scruples to ask anything right out that she wants to know.

"Yes," said Miss Ponsonby softly. "Isn't it wonderful? I could hardly believe it—I am so changed. But he said tonight he had never thought of any other woman. He— he came home to see me. But when I never went anywhere, even when I must know he was home, he thought I didn't want to see him. If I hadn't gone tonight—oh, I owe it all to you two dear girls!"

"When are you to be married?" demanded that terrible Jerry.

"As soon as possible," said Miss Ponsonby. "Stephen was going away next week, but he says he will wait until I can get ready."

"Do you think your father will object this time?" I queried.

"No, I don't think so. Stephen is a rich man now, you know. That wouldn't make any difference with me—but Father is very—practical. Stephen is going to see him tomorrow."

"But what if he does object?" I persisted anxiously.

"The acacia tree will still be there," said Miss Ponsonby firmly.

Their Girl Josie

When Paul Morgan, a rising young lawyer with justifiable political aspirations, married Elinor Ashton, leading woman at the Green Square Theatre, his old schoolmates and neighbours back in Spring Valley held up their hands in horror, and his father and mother up in the weather-grey Morgan homestead were crushed in the depths of humiliation. They had been too proud of Paul ... their only son and such a clever fellow ... and this was their punishment! He had married an actress! To Cyrus and Deborah Morgan, brought up and nourished all their lives on the strictest and straightest of old-fashioned beliefs both as regards this world and that which is to come, this was a tragedy.

They could not be brought to see it in any other light. As their neighbours said, "Cy Morgan never hilt up his head again after Paul married the play-acting woman." But perhaps it was less his humiliation than his sorrow which bowed down his erect form and sprinkled grey in his thick black hair that fifty years had hitherto spared. For Paul, forgetting the sacrifices his mother and father had made for him, had bitterly resented the letter of protest his father had written concerning his marriage. He wrote one angry, unfilial letter back and then came silence. Between grief and shame Cyrus and Deborah Morgan grew old rapidly in the year that followed.

At the end of that time Elinor Morgan, the mother of an hour, died; three months later Paul Morgan was killed in a railroad collision. After the funeral Cyrus

Morgan brought home to his wife their son's little daughter, Joscelyn Morgan.

Her aunt, Annice Ashton, had wanted the baby. Cyrus Morgan had been almost rude in his refusal. His son's daughter should never be brought up by an actress; it was bad enough that her mother had been one and had doubtless transmitted the taint to her child. But in Spring Valley, if anywhere, it might be eradicated.

At first neither Cyrus nor Deborah cared much for Joscelyn. They resented her parentage, her strange, un-Morgan-like name, and the pronounced resemblance she bore to the dark-haired, dark-eyed mother they had never seen. All the Morgans had been fair. If Joscelyn had had Paul's blue eyes and golden curls her grandfather and grandmother would have loved her sooner.

But the love came ... it had to. No living mortal could have resisted Joscelyn. She was the most winsome and lovable little mite of babyhood that ever toddled. Her big dark eyes overflowed with laughter before she could speak, her puckered red mouth broke constantly into dimples and cooing sounds. She had ways that no orthodox Spring Valley baby ever thought of having. Every smile was a caress, every gurgle of attempted speech a song. Her grandparents came to worship her and were stricter than ever with her by reason of their love. Because she was so dear to them she must be saved from her mother's blood.

Joscelyn shot up through a roly-poly childhood into slim, bewitching girlhood in a chill repressive atmosphere. Cyrus and Deborah were nothing if not thorough. The name of Joscelyn's mother was never mentioned to her; she was never called anything but Josie, which sounded more "Christian-like" than Joscelyn; and all the flowering out of her alien beauty was repressed as far as might be in the plainest and dullest of dresses and the primmest arrangement possible to riotous ripe-brown curls.

The girl was never allowed to visit her Aunt Annice,

although frequently invited. Miss Ashton, however, wrote to her occasionally, and every Christmas sent a box of presents which even Cyrus and Deborah Morgan could not forbid her to accept, although they looked with disapproving eyes and ominously set lips at the dainty, frivolous trifles the actress woman sent. They would have liked to cast those painted fans and lace frills and beflounced lingerie into the fire as if they had been infected rags from a pest-house.

The path thus set for Joscelyn's dancing feet to walk in was indeed sedate and narrow. She was seldom allowed to mingle with the young people of even quiet, harmless Spring Valley; she was never allowed to attend local concerts, much less take part in them; she was forbidden to read novels, and Cyrus Morgan burned an old copy of Shakespeare which Paul had given him years ago and which he had himself read and treasured, lest its perusal should awaken unlawful instincts in Joscelyn's heart. The girl's passion for reading was so marked that her grandparents felt that it was their duty to repress it as far as lay in their power.

But Joscelyn's vitality was such that all her bonds and bands served but little to check or retard the growth of her rich nature. Do what they might they could not make a Morgan of her. Her every step was a dance, her every word and gesture full of a grace and virility that filled the old folks with uneasy wonder. She seemed to them charged with dangerous tendencies all the more potent from repression. She was sweet-tempered and sunny, truthful and modest, but she was as little like the trim, simple Spring Valley girls as a crimson rose is like a field daisy, and her unlikeness bore heavily on her grandparents.

Yet they loved her and were proud of her. "Our girl Josie," as they called her, was more to them than they would have admitted even to themselves, and in the main they were satisfied with her, although the grandmother grumbled because Josie did not take kindly to patchwork and rug-making and the grandfather would fain have toned down that exuberance of beauty and vivacity into the meeker pattern of maidenhood he had been accustomed to.

When Joscelyn was seventeen Deborah Morgan noticed a change in her. The girl became quieter and more brooding, falling at times into strange, idle reveries, with her hands clasped over her knee and her big eyes fixed unseeingly on space; or she would creep away for solitary rambles in the beech wood, going away droopingly and returning with dusky glowing cheeks and a nameless radiance, as of some newly discovered power, shining through every muscle and motion. Mrs. Morgan thought the child needed a tonic and gave her sulphur and molasses.

One day the revelation came. Cyrus and Deborah had driven across the valley to visit their married daughter. Not finding her at home they returned. Mrs. Morgan went into the house while her husband went to the stable. Joscelyn was not in the kitchen, but the grandmother heard the sound of voices and laughter in the sitting room across the hall.

"What company has Josie got?" she wondered, as she opened the hall door and paused for a moment on the threshold to listen. As she listened her old face grew grey and pinched; she turned noiselessly and left the house, and flew to her husband as one distracted.

"Cyrus, Josie is play-acting in the room ... laughing and reciting and going on. I heard her. Oh, I've always feared it would break out in her and it has! Come you and listen to her."

The old couple crept through the kitchen and across the hall to the open parlour door as if they were stalking a thief. Joscelyn's laugh rang out as they did so ... a mocking, triumphant peal. Cyrus and Deborah shivered as if they had heard sacrilege.

Joscelyn had put on a trailing, clinging black skirt which her aunt had sent her a year ago and which she had never been permitted to wear. It transformed her into a woman. She had cast aside her waist of dark plum-coloured homespun and wrapped a silken shawl about herself until only her beautiful arms and shoulders were left bare. Her hair, glossy and brown, with burnished red lights where the rays of the dull autumn sun struck on it through the window, was heaped high on her head and held in place by a fillet of pearl beads. Her cheeks were crimson, her whole body from head to foot instinct and alive with a beauty that to Cyrus and Deborah, as they stood mute with horror in the open doorway, seemed akin to some devilish enchantment.

Joscelyn, rapt away from her surroundings, did not perceive her grandparents. Her face was turned from them and she was addressing an unseen auditor in passionate denunciation. She spoke, moved, posed, gesticulated, with an inborn genius shining through every motion and tone like an illuminating lamp.

"Josie, what are you doing?"

It was Cyrus who spoke, advancing into the room like a stern, hard impersonation of judgment. Joscelyn's outstretched arm fell to her side and she turned sharply around; fear came into her face and the light went out of it. A moment before she had been a woman, splendid, unafraid; now she was again the schoolgirl, too confused and shamed to speak.

"What are you doing, Josie?" asked her grandfather again, "dressed up in that indecent manner and talking and twisting to yourself?"

Joscelyn's face, that had grown pale, flamed scarlet again. She lifted her head proudly.

"I was trying Aunt Annice's part in her new play," she answered. "I have not been doing anything wrong, Grandfather."

"Wrong! It's your mother's blood coming out in you, girl, in spite of all our care! Where did you get that play?"

"Aunt Annice sent it to me," answered Joscelyn, casting a quick glance at the book on the table. Then, when her grandfather picked it up gingerly, as if he feared contamination, she added quickly, "Oh, give it to me, please, Grandfather. Don't take it away."

"I am going to burn it," said Cyrus Morgan sternly.

"Oh, don't, Grandfather," cried Joscelyn, with a sob in her voice. "Don't burn it, please. I ... I ... won't practise out of it any more. I'm sorry I've displeased you. Please give me my book."

"No," was the stern reply. "Go to your room, girl, and take off that rig. There is to be no more play-acting in my house, remember that."

He flung the book into the fire that was burning in the grate. For the first time in her life Joscelyn flamed out into passionate defiance.

"You are cruel and unjust, Grandfather. I have done no wrong ... it is not doing wrong to develop the one gift I have. It's the only thing I can do ... and I am going to do it. My mother was an actress and a good woman. So is Aunt Annice. So I mean to be."

"Oh, Josie, Josie," said her grandmother in a scared voice. Her grandfather only repeated sternly, "Go, take that rig off, girl, and let us hear no more of this."

Joscelyn went but she left consternation behind her. Cyrus and Deborah could not have been more shocked if they had discovered the girl robbing her grandfather's desk. They talked the matter over bitterly at the kitchen hearth that night.

"We haven't been strict enough with the girl, Mother," said Cyrus angrily. "We'll have to be stricter if we don't want to have her disgracing us. Did you hear how she defied me? 'So I mean to be,' she says. Mother, we'll have trouble with that girl yet."

"Don't be too harsh with her, Pa ... it'll maybe only drive her to worse," sobbed Deborah.

"I ain't going to be harsh. What I do is for her own good, you know that, Mother. Josie is as dear to me as she is to you, but we've got to be stricter with her."

They were. From that day Josie was watched and distrusted. She was never permitted to be alone. There were no more solitary walks. She felt herself under the surveillance of cold, unsympathetic eyes every moment and her very soul writhed. Joscelyn Morgan, the high-spirited daughter of high-spirited parents, could not long submit to such treatment. It might have passed with a child; to a woman, thrilling with life and conscious power to her very fingertips, it was galling beyond measure. Joscelyn rebelled, but she did nothing secretly ... that was not her nature. She wrote to her Aunt Annice, and when she received her reply she went straight and fearlessly to her grandparents with it.

"Grandfather, this letter is from my aunt. She wishes me to go and live with her and prepare for the stage. I told her I wished to do so. I am going."

Cyrus and Deborah looked at her in mute dismay.

"I know you despise the profession of an actress," the girl went on with heightened colour. "I am sorry you think so about it because it is the only one open to me. I must go ... I must."

"Yes, you must," said Cyrus cruelly. "It's in your blood ... your bad blood, girl."

"My blood isn't bad," cried Joscelyn proudly. "My mother was a sweet, true, good woman. You are unjust, Grandfather. But I don't want you to be angry with me. I love you both and I am very grateful indeed for all your kindness to me. I wish that you could understand what...."

"We understand enough," interrupted Cyrus harshly. "This is all I have to say. Go to your play-acting aunt if you want to. Your grandmother and me won't hinder you. But you'll come back here no more. We'll have nothing further to do with you. You can choose your own way and walk in it."

With this dictum Joscelyn went from Spring Valley. She clung to Deborah and wept at parting, but Cyrus did not even say goodbye to her. On the morning of her departure he went away on business and did not return until evening.

* * *

Joscelyn went on the stage. Her aunt's influence and her mother's fame helped her much. She missed the hard experiences that come to the unassisted beginner. But her own genius must have won in any case. She had all her mother's gifts, deepened by her inheritance of Morgan intensity and sincerity ... much, too, of the Morgan firmness of will. When Joscelyn Morgan was twenty-two she was famous over two continents.

When Cyrus Morgan returned home on the evening after his granddaughter's departure he told his wife that she was never to mention the girl's name in his hearing again. Deborah obeyed. She thought her husband was right, albeit she might in her own heart deplore the necessity of such a decree. Joscelyn had disgraced them; could that be forgiven?

Nevertheless both the old people missed her terribly. The house seemed to have lost its soul with that vivid, ripely tinted young life. They got their married daughter's oldest girl, Pauline, to come and stay with them. Pauline was a quiet, docile maiden, industrious and commonplace—just such a girl as they had vainly striven to make of Joscelyn, to whom Pauline had always been held up as a model. Yet neither Cyrus nor Deborah took to her, and they let her go unregretfully when they found that she wished to return home.

"She hasn't any of Josie's gimp," was old Cyrus's unspoken fault. Deborah spoke, but all she said was, "Polly's a good girl, Father, only she hasn't any snap."

Joscelyn wrote to Deborah occasionally, telling her freely of her plans and doings. If it hurt the girl that no notice was ever taken of her letters she still wrote them. Deborah read the letters grimly and then left them in Cyrus's way. Cyrus would not read them at first; later on he read them stealthily when Deborah was out of the house.

When Joscelyn began to succeed she sent to the old farmhouse papers and magazines containing her photographs and criticisms of her plays and acting. Deborah cut them out and kept them in her upper bureau drawer with Joscelyn's letters. Once she overlooked one and Cyrus found it when he was kindling the fire. He got the scissors and cut it out carefully. A month later Deborah discovered it between the leaves of the family Bible.

But Joscelyn's name was never mentioned between them, and when other people asked them concerning her their replies were cold and ungracious. In a way they had relented towards her, but their shame of her remained. They could never forget that she was an actress.

Once, six years after Joscelyn had left Spring Valley, Cyrus, who was reading a paper by the table, got up with an angry exclamation and stuffed it into the stove, thumping the lid on over it with grim malignity.

"That fool dunno what he's talking about," was all he would say. Deborah had her share of curiosity. The paper was the *National Gazette* and she knew that their next-door neighbour, James Pennan, took it. She went over that evening and borrowed it, saying that their own had been burned before she had had time to read the serial in it. With one exception she read all its columns carefully without finding anything to explain her husband's anger. Then she doubtfully plunged into the exception ... a column of "Stage Notes." Halfway down she came upon an adverse criticism of Joscelyn Morgan and her new play. It was malicious and vituperative. Deborah Morgan's old eyes sparkled dangerously as she read it.

"I guess somebody is pretty jealous of Josie," she muttered. "I don't wonder Pa was riled up. But I guess she can hold her own. She's a Morgan."

No long time after this Cyrus took a notion he'd like a trip to the city. He'd like to see the Horse Fair and look up Cousin Hiram Morgan's folks.

"Hiram and me used to be great chums, Mother. And we're getting kind of mossy, I guess, never stirring out of Spring Valley. Let's go and dissipate for a week—what say?"

Deborah agreed readily, albeit of late years she had been much averse to going far from home and had never at any time been very fond of Cousin Hiram's wife. Cyrus was as pleased as a child over their trip. On the second day of their sojourn in the city he slipped away when Deborah had gone shopping with Mrs. Hiram and hurried through the streets to the Green Square Theatre with a hang-dog look. He bought a ticket apologetically and sneaked in to his seat. It was a matinee performance, and Joscelyn Morgan was starring in her famous new play.

Cyrus waited for the curtain to rise, feeling as if every one of his Spring Valley neighbours must know where he was and revile him for it. If Deborah were ever to find out ... but Deborah must never find out! For the first time in their married life the old man deliberately plotted to deceive his old wife. He must see his girl Josie just once; it was a terrible thing that she was an actress, but she was a successful one, nobody could deny that, except fools who yapped in the *National Gazette*.

The curtain went up and Cyrus rubbed his eyes. He had certainly braced his nerves to behold some mystery of iniquity; instead he saw an old kitchen so like his own at home that it bewildered him; and there, sitting by the cheery wood stove, in homespun gown, with primly braided hair, was Joscelyn—his girl Josie, as he had seen her a thousand times by his own ingle-side. The building rang with applause; one old man pulled out a red bandanna and wiped tears of joy and pride from his eyes. She hadn't changed—Josie hadn't changed. Play-acting hadn't spoiled her—couldn't spoil her. Wasn't she Paul's daughter! And all this applause was for her—for Josie.

Joscelyn's new play was a homely, pleasant production with rollicking comedy and heart-moving pathos skilfully commingled. Joscelyn pervaded it all with a convincing simplicity that was really the triumph of art. Cyrus Morgan listened and exulted in her; at every burst of applause his eyes gleamed with pride. He wanted to go on the stage and box the ears of the villain who plotted against her; he wanted to shake hands with the good woman who stood by her; he wanted to pay off the mortgage and make Josie happy. He wiped tears from his eyes in the third act when Josie was turned out of doors and, when the fourth left her a happy, blushing bride, hand in hand with her farmer lover, he could have wept again for joy.

Cyrus Morgan went out into the daylight feeling as if he had awakened from a dream. At the outer door he came upon Mrs. Hiram and Deborah. Deborah's face was stained with tears, and she caught at his hand.

"Oh, Pa, wasn't it splendid—wasn't our girl Josie splendid! I'm so proud of her. Oh, I was bound to hear her. I was afraid you'd be mad, so I didn't let on and when I saw you in the seat down there I couldn't believe my eyes. Oh, I've just been crying the whole time. Wasn't it splendid! Wasn't our girl Josie splendid?"

The crowd around looked at the old pair with amused, indulgent curiosity, but they were quite oblivious to their surroundings, even to Mrs. Hiram's anxiety to decoy them away. Cyrus Morgan cleared his throat and said, "It was great, Mother, great. She took the shine off the other play-actors all right. I knew that *National Gazette* man didn't know what he was talking about. Mother, let us go and see Josie right off. She's stopping with her aunt at the Maberly Hotel—I saw it in the paper this morning. I'm going to tell her she was right and we were wrong. Josie's beat them all, and I'm going to tell her so!"

A Millionaire's Proposal

Thrush Hill, Oct. 5, 18—.

It is all settled at last, and in another week I shall have left Thrush Hill. I am a little bit sorry and a great bit glad. I am going to Montreal to spend the winter with Alicia.

Alicia—it used to be plain Alice when she lived at Thrush Hill and made her own dresses and trimmed her own hats—is my half-sister. She is eight years older than I am. We are both orphans, and Aunt Elizabeth brought us up here at Thrush Hill, the most delightful old country place in the world, half smothered in big willows and poplars, every one of which I have climbed in the early tomboy days of gingham pinafores and sun-bonnets.

When Alicia was eighteen she married Roger Gresham, a man of forty. The world said that she married him for his money. I dare say she did. Alicia was tired of poverty.

I don't blame her. Very likely I shall do the same thing one of these days, if I get the chance—for I too am tired of poverty.

When Alicia went to Montreal she wanted to take me with her, but I wanted to be outdoors, romping in the hay or running wild in the woods with Jack.

Jack Willoughby—Dr. John H. Willoughby, it reads on his office door—was the son of our nearest neighbour. We were chums always, and when he went away to college I was heartbroken.

The vacations were the only joy of my life then.

I don't know just when I began to notice a change in Jack, but when he came home two years ago, a full-fledged M.D.—a great, tall, broad-shouldered fellow, with the sweetest moustache, and lovely thick black hair, just made for poking one's fingers through—I realized it to the full. Jack was grown up. The dear old days of bird-nesting and nutting and coasting and fishing and general delightful goings-on were over forever.

I was sorry at first. I wanted "Jack." "Dr. Willoughby" seemed too distinguished and far away.

I suppose he found a change in me, too. I had put on long skirts and wore my hair up. I had also found out that I had a complexion, and that sunburn was not becoming. I honestly thought I looked pretty, but Jack surveyed me with decided disapprobation.

"What have you done to yourself? You don't look like the same girl. I'd never know you in that rig-out, with all those flippery-trippery curls all over your head. Why don't you comb your hair straight back, and let it hang in a braided tail, like you used to?"

This didn't suit me at all. When I expect a compliment and get something quite different I always get snippy. So I said, with what I intended to be crushing dignity, "that I supposed I wasn't the same girl; I had grown up, and if he didn't like my curls he needn't look at them. For my part, I thought them infinitely preferable to that horrid, conceited-looking moustache he had grown."

"I'll shave it off if it doesn't suit you," said Jack amiably.

Jack is always so provokingly good-humoured. When you've taken pains and put yourself out—even to the extent of fibbing about a moustache—to exasperate a person, there is nothing more annoying than to have him keep perfectly angelic.

But after a while Jack and I adjusted ourselves to the change in each other and became very good friends again. It was quite a different friendship from the old, but it was very pleasant. Yes, it was; I *will* admit that much.

I was provoked at Jack's determination to settle down for life in Valleyfield, a horrible, humdrum, little country village.

"You'll never make your fortune there, Jack," I said spitefully. "You'll just be a poor, struggling country doctor all your life, and you'll be grey at forty."

"I don't expect to make a fortune, Kitty," said Jack quietly. "Do you think that is the one desirable thing? I shall never be a rich man. But riches are not the only thing that makes life pleasant."

"Well, I think they have a good deal to do with it, anyhow," I retorted. "It's all very well to pretend to despise wealth, but it's generally a case of sour grapes. *I* will own up honestly that I'd *love* to be rich."

It always seems to make Jack blue and grumpy when I talk like that. I suppose that is one reason why he never asked me to settle down in life as a country doctor's wife. Another was, no doubt, that I always nipped his sentimental sproutings religiously in the bud.

Three weeks ago Alicia wrote to me, asking me to spend the winter with her. Her letters always make me just gasp with longing for the life they describe.

Jack's face, when I told him about it, was so woebegone that I felt a stab of remorse, even in the heyday of my delight.

"Do you really mean it, Kitty? Are you going away to leave me?"

"You won't miss me much," I said flippantly—I had a creepy, crawly presentiment that a scene of some kind was threatening—"and I'm awfully tired of Thrush Hill and country life, Jack. I suppose it is horribly ungrateful of me to say so, but it is the truth."

"I shall miss you," he said soberly.

Somehow he had my hands in his. *How* did he ever get them? I was sure I had them safely tucked out of harm's way behind me. "You know, Kitty, that I love you. I am a poor man—perhaps I may never be anything else—and this may seem to you very presumptuous. But I cannot let you go like this. Will you be my wife, dear?"

Wasn't it horribly straightforward and direct? So like Jack! I tried to pull my hands away, but he held them fast. There was nothing to do but answer him. That "no" I had determined to say must be said, but, oh! how woefully it did stick in my throat!

And I honestly believe that by the time I got it out it would have been transformed into a "yes," in spite of me, had it not been for a certain paragraph in Alicia's letter which came providentially to my mind:

Not to flatter you, Katherine, you are a beauty, my dear—if your photo is to be trusted. If you have not discovered that fact before—how should you, indeed, in a place like Thrush Hill?—you soon will in Montreal. With your face and figure you will make a sensation.

There is to be a nephew of the Sinclairs here this winter. He is an American, immensely wealthy, and will be the catch of the season. A word to the wise, etc. Don't get into any foolish entanglement down there. I have heard some gossip of you and our old playfellow, Jack Willoughby. I hope it is nothing but gossip. You can do better than that, Katherine.

That settled Jack's fate, if there ever had been any doubt.

"Don't talk like that, Jack," I said hurriedly. "It is all nonsense. I think a great deal of you as a friend and—and—all that, you know. But I can never marry you."

"Are you sure, Kitty?" said Jack earnestly. "Don't you care for me at all?"

It was horrid of Jack to ask that question!

"No," I said miserably, "not—not in that way, Jack. Oh, don't ever say anything like this to me again."

He let go of my hands then, white to the lips.

"Oh, don't look like that, Jack," I entreated.

"I can't help it," he said in a low voice. "But I won't bother you again, dear. It was foolish of me to expect—to hope for anything of the sort. You are a thousand times too good for me, I know."

"Oh, indeed I'm not, Jack," I protested. "If you knew

how horrid I am, really, you'd be glad and thankful for your escape. Oh, Jack, I wish people never grew up."

Jack smiled sadly.

"Don't feel badly over this, Kitty. It isn't your fault. Good night, dear."

He turned my face up and kissed me squarely on the mouth. He had never kissed me since the summer before he went away to college. Somehow it didn't seem a bit the same as it used to; it was—nicer now.

After he went away I came upstairs and had a good, comfortable howl. Then I buried the whole affair decently. I am not going to think of it any more.

I shall always have the highest esteem for Jack, and I hope he will soon find some nice girl who will make him happy. Mary Carter would jump at him, I know. To be sure, she is as homely as she can be and live. But, then, Jack is always telling me how little he cares for beauty, so I have no doubt she will suit him admirably.

As for myself—well, I am ambitious. I don't suppose my ambition is a very lofty one, but such as it is I mean to hunt it down. Come. Let me put it down in black and white, once for all, and see how it looks:

I mean to marry the rich nephew of the Sinclairs.

There! It is out, and I feel better. How mercenary and awful it looks written out in cold blood like that. I wouldn't have Jack or Aunt Elizabeth—dear, unworldly old soul—see it for the world. But I wouldn't mind Alicia.

Poor dear Jack!

* * *

Montreal, Dec. 16, 18—.

This is a nice way to keep a journal. But the days when I could write regularly are gone by. That was when I was at Thrush Hill.

I am having a simply divine time. How in the world did I ever contrive to live at Thrush Hill?

To be sure, I felt badly enough that day in October

when I left it. When the train left Valleyfield I just cried like a baby.

Alicia and Roger welcomed me very heartily, and after the first week of homesickness—I shiver yet when I think of it—was over, I settled down to my new life as if I had been born to it.

Alicia has a magnificent home and everything heart could wish for—jewels, carriages, servants, opera boxes, and social position. Roger is a model husband apparently. I must also admit that he is a model brother-in-law.

I could feel Alicia looking me over critically the moment we met. I trembled with suspense, but I was soon relieved.

"Do you know, Katherine, I am glad to see that your photograph didn't flatter you. Photographs so often do, I am positively surprised at the way you have developed, my dear; you used to be such a scrawny little brown thing. By the way, I hope there is nothing between you and Jack Willoughby?"

"No, of course not," I answered hurriedly. I had intended to tell Alicia all about Jack, but when it came to the point I couldn't.

"I am glad of that," said Alicia, with a relieved air. "Of course, I've no doubt Jack is a good fellow enough. He was a nice boy. But he would not be a suitable husband for you, Katherine."

I knew that very well. That was just why I had refused him. But it made me wince to hear Alicia say it. I instantly froze up—Alicia says dignity is becoming to me—and Jack's name has never been mentioned between us since.

I made my bow to society at an "At Home" which Alicia gave for that purpose. She drilled me well beforehand, and I think I acquitted myself decently. Charlie Vankleek, whose verdict makes or mars every debutante in his set, has approved of me. He called me a beauty, and everybody now believes that I am one, and greets me accordingly.

I met Gus Sinclair at Mrs. Brompton's dinner. Alicia

declares it was a case of love at first sight. If so, I must confess that it was all on one side.

Mr. Sinclair is undeniably ugly—even Alicia has to admit that—and can't hold a candle to Jack in point of looks, for Jack, poor boy, was handsome, if he were nothing else. But, as Alicia does not fail to remind me, Mr. Sinclair's homeliness is well gilded.

Apart from his appearance, I really liked him very much. He is a gentlemanly little fellow—his head reaches about to my shoulder—cultured and travelled, and can talk splendidly, which Jack never could.

He took me into dinner at Mrs. Brompton's, and was very attentive. You may imagine how many angelic glances I received from the other candidates for his favour.

Since then I have been having the gayest time imaginable. Dances, dinners, luncheons, afternoon teas, "functions" to no end, and all delightful.

Aunt Elizabeth writes to me, but I have never heard a word from Jack. He seems to have forgotten my existence completely. No doubt he has consoled himself with Mary Carter.

Well, that is all for the best, but I must say I did not think Jack could have forgotten me so soon or so absolutely. Of course it does not make the least difference to me.

The Sinclairs and the Bromptons and the Curries are to dine here tonight. I can see myself reflected in the long mirror before me, and I really think my appearance will satisfy even Gus Sinclair's critical eye. I am pale, as usual, I never have any colour. That used to be one of Jack's grievances. He likes pink and white milkmaidish girls. My "magnificent pallor" didn't suit him at all.

But, what is more to the purpose, it suits Gus Sinclair. He admires the statuesque style.

* * *

Montreal, Jan. 20, 18—.

Here it is a whole month since my last entry. I am sitting here decked out in "gloss of satin and glimmer of pearls" for Mrs. Currie's dance. These few minutes, after I emerge from the hands of my maid and before the carriage is announced, are almost the only ones I ever have to myself.

I am having a good time still. Somehow, though, it isn't as exciting as it used to be. I'm afraid I'm very changeable. I believe I must be homesick.

I'd love to get a glimpse of dear old Thrush Hill and Aunt Elizabeth, and J—but, no! I will not write that.

Mr. Sinclair has not spoken yet, but there is no doubt that he soon will. Of course, I shall accept him when he does, and I coolly told Alicia so when she just as coolly asked me what I meant to do.

"Certainly, I shall marry him," I said crossly, for the subject always irritates me. "Haven't I been laying myself out all winter to catch him? That is the bold, naked truth, and ugly enough it is. My dearly beloved sister, I mean to accept Mr. Sinclair, without any hesitation, whenever I get the chance."

"I give you credit for more sense than to dream of doing anything else," said Alicia in relieved tones. "Katherine, you are a very lucky girl."

"Because I am going to marry a rich man for his money?" I said coldly.

Sometimes I get snippy with Alicia these days.

"No," said my half-sister in an exasperated way. "Why will you persist in speaking in that way? You are very provoking. It is not likely I would wish to see you throw yourself away on a poor man, and I'm sure you must like Gus."

"Oh, yes, I like him well enough," I said listlessly. "To be sure, I did think once, in my salad days, that liking wasn't quite all in an affair of this kind. I was absurd enough to imagine that love had something to do with it."

"Don't talk so nonsensically," said Alicia sharply.

"Love! Well, of course, you ought to love your husband, and you will. He loves you enough, at all events."

"Alicia," I said earnestly, looking her straight in the face and speaking bluntly enough to have satisfied even Jack's love of straightforwardness, "you married for money and position, so people say. Are you happy?"

For the first time that I remembered, Alicia blushed. She was very angry.

"Yes, I did marry for money," she said sharply, "and I don't regret it. Thank heaven, I never was a fool."

"Don't be vexed, Alicia," I entreated. "I only asked because—well, it is no matter."

* * *

Montreal, Jan. 25, 18—.

It is bedtime, but I am too excited and happy and miserable to sleep. Jack has been here—dear old Jack! How glad I was to see him.

His coming was so unexpected. I was sitting alone in my room this afternoon—I believe I was moping—when Bessie brought up his card. I gave it one rapturous look and tore downstairs, passing Alicia in the hall like a whirlwind, and burst into the drawing-room in a most undignified way.

"Jack!" I cried, holding out both hands to him in welcome.

There he was, just the same old Jack, with his splendid big shoulders and his lovely brown eyes. And his necktie was crooked, too; as soon as I could get my hands free I put them up and straightened it out for him. How nice and old-timey that was!

"So you are glad to see me, Kitty?" he said as he squeezed my hands in his big strong paws.

"'Deed and 'deed I am, Jack. I thought you had forgotten me altogether. And I've been so homesick and so—so everything," I said incoherently. "And, oh, Jack, I've so many questions to ask I don't know where to begin. Tell me all the Thrush Hill and Valleyfield news, tell me everything that has happened since I left. How many people have you killed off? And, oh, why didn't you come to see me before?"

"I didn't think I should be wanted, Kitty," Jack answered quietly. "You seemed to be so absorbed in your new life that old friends and interests were crowded out."

"So I was at first," I answered penitently. "I was dazzled, you know. The glare was too much for my Thrush Hill brown. But it's different now. How did you happen to come, Jack?"

"I had to come to Montreal on business, and I thought it would be too bad if I went back without coming to see what they had been doing in Vanity Fair to my little playmate."

"Well, what do you think they have been doing?" I asked saucily.

I had on a particularly fetching gown and knew I was looking my best. Jack, however, looked me over with his head on one side.

"Well, I don't know, Kitty," he said slowly. "That is a stunning sort of dress you have on—not so pretty, though, as that old blue muslin you used to wear last summer—and your hair is pretty good. But you look rather disdainful and, after all, I believe I prefer Thrush Hill Kitty."

How like Jack that was. He never thought me really pretty, and he is too honest to pretend he does.

But I didn't care. I just laughed, and we sat down together and had a long, delightful, chummy talk.

Jack told me all the Valleyfield gossip, not forgetting to mention that Mary Carter was going to be married to a minister in June. Jack didn't seem to mind it a bit, so I guess he couldn't have been particularly interested in Mary.

In due time Alicia sailed in. I suppose she had found out from Bessie who my caller was, and felt rather worried over the length of our tête-à-tête.

She greeted Jack very graciously, but with a certain

polite condescension of which she is past mistress. I am sure Jack felt it, for, as soon as he decently could, he got up to go. Alicia asked him to remain to dinner.

"We are having a few friends to dine with us, but it is quite an informal affair," she said sweetly.

I felt that Jack glanced at me for the fraction of a second. But I remembered that Gus Sinclair was coming too, and I did not look at him.

Then he declined quietly. He had a business engagement, he said.

I suppose Alicia had noticed that look at me, for she showed her claws.

"Don't forget to call any time you are in Montreal," she said more sweetly than ever. "I am sure Katherine will always be glad to see any of her old friends, although some of her new ones *are* proving very absorbing—one, in especial. Don't blush, Katherine, I am sure Mr. Willoughby won't tell any tales out of school to your old Valleyfield friends."

I was not blushing, and I was furious. It was really too bad of Alicia, although I don't see why I need have cared.

Alicia kept her eye on us both until Jack was fairly gone. Then she remarked in the patronizing tone which I detest:

"Really, Katherine, Jack Willoughby has developed into quite a passable-looking fellow, although he is rather shabby. But I suppose he is poor."

"Yes," I answered curtly, "he is poor, in everything except youth and manhood and goodness and truth! But I suppose those don't count for anything."

Whereupon Alicia lifted her eyebrows and looked me over.

Just at dusk a box arrived with Jack's compliments. It was full of lovely white carnations, and must have cost the extravagant fellow more than he has any business to waste on flowers. I was beast enough to put them on when I went down to listen to another man's love-making.

This evening I sparkled and scintillated with unusual

brilliancy, for Jack's visit and my consequent crossing of swords with Alicia had produced a certain elation of spirits. When Gus Sinclair was leaving he asked if he might see me alone tomorrow afternoon.

I knew what that meant, and a cold shiver went up and down my backbone. But I looked down at him—spick-and-span and glossy—*his* neckties are never crooked—and said, yes, he might come at three o'clock.

Alicia had noticed our aside—when did anything ever escape her?—and when he was gone she asked, significantly, what secret he had been telling me.

"He wants to see me alone tomorrow afternoon. I suppose you know what that means, Alicia?"

"Ah," purred Alicia, "I congratulate you, my dear."

"Aren't your congratulations a little premature?" I asked coldly. "I haven't accepted him yet."

"But you will?"

"Oh, certainly. Isn't it what we've schemed and angled for? I'm very well satisfied."

And so I am. But I wish it hadn't come so soon after Jack's visit, because I feel rather upset yet. Of course I like Gus Sinclair very much, and I am sure I shall be very fond of him.

Well, I must go to bed now and get my beauty sleep. I don't want to be haggard and hollow-eyed at that important interview tomorrow—an interview that will decide my destiny.

* * *

Thrush Hill, May 6, 18—.

Well, it did decide it, but not exactly in the way I anticipated. I can look back on the whole affair quite calmly now, but I wouldn't live it over again for all the wealth of Ind.

That day when Gus Sinclair came I was all ready for him. I had put on my very prettiest new gown to do honour to the occasion, and Alicia smilingly assured me I was looking very well.

"And *so* cool and composed. Will you be able to keep

that up? Don't you really feel a little nervous, Katherine?"

"Not in the least," I said. "I suppose I ought to be, according to traditions, but I never felt less flustered in my life."

When Bessie brought up Gus Sinclair's card Alicia dropped a pecky little kiss on my cheek, and pushed me toward the door. I went down calmly, although I'll admit that my heart *was* beating wildly. Gus Sinclair was plainly nervous, but I was composed enough for both. You would really have thought that I was in the habit of being proposed to by a millionaire every day.

"I suppose you know what I have come to say," he said, standing before me, as I leaned gracefully back in a big chair, having taken care that the folds of my dress fell just as they should.

And then he proceeded to say it in a rather jumbled-up fashion, but very sincerely.

I remember thinking at the time that he must have composed the speech in his head the night before, and rehearsed it several times, but was forgetting it in spots.

When he ended with the self-same question that Jack had asked me three months before at Thrush Hill he stopped and took my hands.

I looked up at him. His good, homely face was close to mine, and in his eyes was an unmistakable look of love and tenderness.

I opened my mouth to say yes.

And then there came over me in one rush the most awful realization of the sacrilege I was going to commit.

I forgot everything except that I loved Jack Willoughby, and that I could never, never marry anybody in the world except him.

Then I pulled my hands away and burst into hysterical, undignified tears.

"I beg your pardon," said Mr. Sinclair. "I did not mean to startle you. Have I been too abrupt? Surely you must have known—you must have expected—"

"Yes—yes—I knew," I cried miserably, "and I intended

right up to this very minute to marry you. I'm so sorry—but I can't—I can't."

"I don't understand," he said in a bewildered tone. "If you expected it, then why—why—don't you care for me?"

"No, that's just it," I sobbed. "I don't love you at all—and I do love somebody else. But he is poor, and I hate poverty. So I refused him, and I meant to marry you just because you are rich."

Such a pained look came over his face. "I did not think this of you," he said in a low tone.

"Oh, I know I have acted shamefully," I said. "You can't think any worse of me than I do of myself. How you must despise me!"

"No," he said, with a grim smile, "if I did it would be easier for me. I might not love you then. Don't distress yourself, Katherine. I do not deny that I feel greatly hurt and disappointed, but I am glad you have been true to yourself at last. Don't cry, dear."

"You're very good," I answered disconsolately, "but all the same the fact remains that I have behaved disgracefully to you, and I know you think so. Oh, Mr. Sinclair, please, please, go away. I feel so miserably ashamed of myself that I cannot look you in the face."

"I am going, dear," he said gently. "I know all this must be very painful to you, but it is not easy for me, either."

"Can you forgive me?" I said wistfully.

"Yes, my dear, completely. Do not let yourself be unhappy over this. Remember that I will always be your friend. Goodbye."

He held out his hand and gave mine an earnest clasp. Then he went away.

I remained in the drawing-room, partly because I wanted to finish out my cry, and partly because, miserable coward that I was, I didn't dare face Alicia. Finally she came in, her face wreathed with anticipatory smiles. But when her eyes fell on my forlorn, crumpled self she fairly jumped.

"Katherine, what is the matter?" she asked sharply. "Didn't Mr. Sinclair—"

"Yes, he did," I said desperately. "And I've refused him. There now, Alicia!"

Then I waited for the storm to burst. It didn't all at once. The shock was too great, and at first quite paralyzed my half-sister.

"Katherine," she gasped, "are you crazy? Have you lost your senses?"

"No, I've just come to them. It's true enough, Alicia. You can scold all you like. I know I deserve it, and I won't flinch. I did really intend to take him, but when it came to the point I couldn't. I didn't love him."

Then, indeed, the storm burst. I never saw Alicia so angry before, and I never got so roundly abused. But even Alicia has her limits, and at last she grew calmer.

"You have behaved disgracefully," she concluded. "I am disgusted with you. You have encouraged Gus Sinclair markedly right along, and now you throw him over like this. I never dreamed that you were capable of such unwomanly behaviour."

"That's a hard word, Alicia," I protested feebly.

She dealt me a withering glance. "It does not begin to be as hard as your shameful conduct merits. To think of losing a fortune like that for the sake of sentimental folly! I didn't think you were such a consummate fool."

"I suppose you absorbed all the sense of our family," I said drearily. "There now, Alicia, do leave me alone. I'm down in the very depths already."

"What do you mean to do now?" said Alicia scornfully. "Go back to Valleyfield and marry that starving country doctor of yours, I suppose?"

I flared up then; Alicia might abuse me all she liked, but I wasn't going to hear a word against Jack.

"Yes, I will, if he'll have me," I said, and I marched out of the room and upstairs, with my head very high.

Of course I decided to leave Montreal as soon as I could. But I couldn't get away within a week, and it was a very unpleasant one. Alicia treated me with icy indifference, and I knew I should never be reinstated in her good graces.

To my surprise, Roger took my part. "Let the girl alone," he told Alicia. "If she doesn't love Sinclair, she was right in refusing him. I, for one, am glad that she has got enough truth and womanliness in her to keep her from selling herself."

Then he came to the library where I was moping, and laid his hand on my head.

"Little girl," he said earnestly, "no matter what anyone says to you, never marry a man for his money or for any other reason on earth except because you love him."

This comforted me greatly, and I did not cry myself to sleep that night as usual.

At last I got away. I had telegraphed to Jack: "Am coming home Wednesday; meet me at train," and I knew he would be there. How I longed to see him again—dear, old, badly treated Jack.

I got to Valleyfield just at dusk. It was a rainy evening, and everything was slush and fog and gloom. But away up I saw the home light at Thrush Hill, and Jack was waiting for me on the platform.

"Oh, Jack!" I said, clinging to him, regardless of appearances. "Oh, I'm so glad to be back."

"That's right, Kitty. I knew you wouldn't forget us. How well you are looking!"

"I suppose I ought to be looking wretched," I said penitently. "I've been behaving very badly, Jack. Wait till we get away from the crowd and I'll tell you all about it."

And I did.

I didn't gloss over anything, but just confessed the whole truth. Jack heard me through in silence, and then he kissed me.

"Can you forgive me, Jack, and take me back?" I whispered, cuddling up to him.

And he said—but, on second thought, I will not write down what he said.

We are to be married in June.

A Substitute Journalist

Clifford Baxter came into the sitting-room where Patty was darning stockings and reading a book at the same time. Patty could do things like that. The stockings were well darned too, and Patty understood and remembered what she read.

Clifford flung himself into a chair with a sigh of weariness. "Tired?" queried Patty sympathetically.

"Yes, rather. I've been tramping about the wharves all day gathering longshore items. But, Patty, I've got a chance at last. Tonight as I was leaving the office Mr. Harmer gave me a real assignment for tomorrow—two of them in fact, but only one of importance. I'm to go and interview Mr. Keefe on this new railroad bill that's up before the legislature. He's in town, visiting his old college friend, Mr. Reid, and he's quite big game. I wouldn't have had the assignment, of course, if there'd been anyone else to send, but most of the staff will be away all day tomorrow to see about that mine explosion at Midbury or the teamsters' strike at Bainsville, and I'm the only one available. Harmer gave me a pretty broad hint that it was my chance to win my spurs, and that if I worked up a good article out of it I'd stand a fair show of being taken on permanently next month when Alsop leaves. There'll be a shuffle all round then, you know. Everybody on the staff will be pushed up a peg, and that will leave a vacant space at the foot."

Patty threw down her darning needle and clapped her hands with delight. Clifford gazed at her admiringly, thinking that he had the prettiest sister in the world—she was so bright, so eager, so rosy.

"Oh, Clifford, how splendid!" she exclaimed. "Just as we'd begun to give up hope too. Oh, you must get the position! You must hand in a good write-up. Think what it means to us."

"Yes, I know." Clifford dropped his head on his hand and stared rather moodily at the lamp. "But my joy is chastened, Patty. Of course I want to get the permanency, since it seems to be the only possible thing, but you know my heart isn't really in newspaper work. The plain truth is I don't like it, although I do my best. You know Father always said I was a born mechanic. If I only could get a position somewhere among machinery—that would be my choice. There's one vacant in the Steel and Iron Works at Bancroft—but of course I've no chance of getting it."

"I know. It's too bad," said Patty, returning to her stockings with a sigh. "I wish I were a boy with a foothold on the *Chronicle*. I firmly believe that I'd make a good newspaper woman, if such a thing had ever been heard of in Aylmer."

"That you would. You've twice as much knack in that line as I have. You seem to know by instinct just what to leave out and put in. I never do, and Harmer has to blue-pencil my copy mercilessly. Well, I'll do my best with this, as it's very necessary I should get the permanency, for I fear our family purse is growing very slim. Mother's face has a new wrinkle of worry every day. It hurts me to see it."

"And me," sighed Patty. "I do wish I could find something to do too. If only we both could get positions, everything would be all right. Mother wouldn't have to worry so. Don't say anything about this chance to her until you see what comes of it. She'd only be doubly disappointed if nothing did. What is your other assignment?"

"Oh, I've got to go out to Bancroft on the morning train and write up old Mr. Moreland's birthday celebration. He is a hundred years old, and there's going to be a presentation and speeches and that sort of thing. Nothing very exciting about it. I'll have to come back on the three o'clock train and hurry out to catch my politician before he leaves at five. Take a stroll down to meet my train, Patty. We can go out as far as Mr. Reid's house together, and the walk will do you good."

The Baxters lived in Aylmer, a lively little town with two newspapers, the *Chronicle* and the *Ledger*. Between these two was a sharp journalistic rivalry in the matter of "beats" and "scoops." In the preceding spring Clifford had been taken on the *Chronicle* on trial, as a sort of general handyman. There was no pay attached to the position, but he was getting training and there was the possibility of a permanency in September if he proved his mettle. Mr. Baxter had died two years before, and the failure of the company in which Mrs. Baxter's money was invested had left the little family dependent on their own resources. Clifford, who had cherished dreams of a course in mechanical engineering, knew that he must give them up and go to the first work that offered itself, which he did staunchly and uncomplainingly. Patty, who hitherto had had no designs on a "career," but had been sunnily content to be a home girl and Mother's right hand, also realized that it would be well to look about her for something to do. She was not really needed so far as the work of the little house went, and the whole burden must not be allowed to fall on Clifford's eighteen-year-old shoulders. Patty was his senior by a year, and ready to do her part unflinchingly.

The next afternoon Patty went down to meet Clifford's train. When it came, no Clifford appeared. Patty stared about her at the hurrying throngs in bewilderment. Where was Clifford? Hadn't he come on the train? Surely he must have, for there was no other until seven o'clock. She must have missed him somehow. Patty waited until everybody had left the station, then she walked slowly homeward. As the *Chronicle* office was on her way, she dropped in to see if Clifford had reported there.

She found nobody in the editorial offices except the office boy, Larry Brown, who promptly informed her that not only had Clifford not arrived, but that there was a telegram from him saying that he had missed his train. Patty gasped in dismay. It was dreadful!

"Where is Mr. Harmer?" she asked.

"He went home as soon as the afternoon edition came out. He left before the telegram came. He'll be furious when he finds out that nobody has gone to interview that foxy old politician," said Larry, who knew all about Clifford's assignment and its importance.

"Isn't there anyone else here to go?" queried Patty desperately.

Larry shook his head. "No, there isn't a soul in. We're mighty short-handed just now on account of the explosion and the strike."

Patty went downstairs and stood for a moment in the hall, rapt in reflection. If she had been at home, she verily believed she would have sat down and cried. Oh, it was too bad, too disappointing! Clifford would certainly lose all chance of the permanency, even if the irate news editor did not discharge him at once. What could she do? Could she do anything? She *must* do something.

"If I only could go in his place," moaned Patty softly to herself.

Then she started. Why not? Why not go and interview the big man herself? To be sure, she did not know a great deal about interviewing, still less about railroad bills, and nothing at all about politics. But if she did her best it might be better than nothing, and might at least save Clifford his present hold.

With Patty, to decide was to act. She flew back to the reporters' room, pounced on a pencil and tablet, and hurried off, her breath coming quickly, and her eyes shining with excitement. It was quite a long walk out to Mr. Reid's place and Patty was tired when she got there, but her courage was not a whit abated. She mounted the steps and rang the bell undauntedly.

"Can I see Mr.—Mr.—Mr.—" Patty paused for a

moment in dismay. She had forgotten the name. The maid who had come to the door looked her over so superciliously that Patty flushed with indignation. "The gentleman who is visiting Mr. Reid," she said crisply. "I can't remember his name, but I've come to interview him on behalf of the *Chronicle*. Is he in?"

"If you mean Mr. Reefer, he is," said the maid quite respectfully. Evidently the *Chronicle*'s name carried weight in the Reid establishment. "Please come into the library. I'll go and tell him."

Patty had just time to seat herself at the table, spread out her paper imposingly, and assume a businesslike air when Mr. Reefer came in. He was a tall, handsome old man with white hair, jet-black eyes, and a mouth that made Patty hope she wouldn't stumble on any questions he wouldn't want to answer. Patty knew she would waste her breath if she did. A man with a mouth like that would never tell anything he didn't want to tell.

"Good afternoon. What can I do for you, madam?" inquired Mr. Reefer with the air and tone of a man who means to be courteous, but has no time or information to waste.

Patty was almost overcome by the "Madam." For a moment, she quailed. She couldn't ask that masculine sphinx questions! Then the thought of her mother's pale, careworn face flashed across her mind, and all her courage came back with an inspiriting rush. She bent forward to look eagerly into Mr. Reefer's carved, granite face, and said with a frank smile:

"I have come to interview you on behalf of the *Chronicle* about the railroad bill. It was my brother who had the assignment, but he has missed his train and I have come in his place because, you see, it is so important to us. So much depends on this assignment. Perhaps Mr. Harmer will give Clifford a permanent place on the staff if he turns in a good article about you. He is only handyman now. I just couldn't let him miss the chance—he might never have another. And it means so much to us and Mother."

"Are you a member of the *Chronicle* staff yourself?" inquired Mr. Reefer with a shade more geniality in his tone.

"Oh, no! I've nothing to do with it, so you won't mind my being inexperienced, will you? I don't know just what I should ask you, so won't you please just tell me everything about the bill, and Mr. Harmer can cut out what doesn't matter?"

Mr. Reefer looked at Patty for a few moments with a face about as expressive as a graven image. Perhaps he was thinking about the bill, and perhaps he was thinking what a bright, vivid, plucky little girl this was with her waiting pencil and her air that strove to be businesslike, and only succeeded in being eager and hopeful and anxious.

"I'm not used to being interviewed myself," he said slowly, "so I don't know very much about it. We're both green hands together, I imagine. But I'd like to help you out, so I don't mind telling you what I think about this bill, and its bearing on certain important interests."

Mr. Reefer proceeded to tell her, and Patty's pencil flew as she scribbled down his terse, pithy sentences. She found herself asking questions too, and enjoying it. For the first time, Patty thought she might rather like politics if she understood them—and they did not seem so hard to understand when a man like Mr. Reefer explained them. For half an hour he talked to her, and at the end of that time Patty was in full possession of his opinion on the famous railroad bill in all its aspects.

"There now, I'm talked out," said Mr. Reefer. "You can tell your news editor that you know as much about the railroad bill as Andrew Reefer knows. I hope you'll succeed in pleasing him, and that your brother will get the position he wants. But he shouldn't have missed that train. You tell him that. Boys with important things to do mustn't miss trains. Perhaps it's just as well he did in this case though, but tell him not to let it happen again."

Patty went straight home, wrote up her interview in ship-shape form, and took it down to the *Chronicle* office.

There she found Mr. Harmer, scowling blackly. The little news editor looked to be in a rather bad temper, but he nodded not unkindly to Patty. Mr. Harmer knew the Baxters well and liked them, although he would have sacrificed them all without a qualm for a "scoop."

"Good evening, Patty. Take a chair. That brother of yours hasn't turned up yet. The next time I give him an assignment, he'll manage to be on hand in time to do it."

"Oh," cried Patty breathlessly, "please, Mr. Harmer, I have the interview here. I thought perhaps I could do it in Clifford's place, and I went out to Mr. Reid's and saw Mr. Reefer. He was very kind and—"

"Mr. who?" fairly shouted Mr. Harmer.

"Mr. Reefer—Mr. Andrew Reefer. He told me to tell you that this article contained all he knew or thought about the railroad bill and—"

But Mr. Harmer was no longer listening. He had snatched the neatly written sheets of Patty's report and was skimming over them with a practised eye. Then Patty thought he must have gone crazy. He danced around the office, waving the sheets in the air, and then he dashed frantically up the stairs to the composing room.

Ten minutes later, he returned and shook the mystified Patty by the hand.

"Patty, it's the biggest beat we've ever had! We've scooped not only the *Ledger*, but every other newspaper in the country. How did you do it? How did you ever beguile or bewitch Andrew Reefer into giving you an interview?"

"Why," said Patty in utter bewilderment, "I just went out to Mr. Reid's and asked for the gentleman who was visiting there—I'd forgotten his name—and Mr. Reefer came down and I told him my brother had been detailed to interview him on behalf of the *Chronicle* about the bill, and that Clifford had missed his train, and wouldn't he let me interview him in his place and excuse my inexperience—and he did."

"It wasn't Andrew Reefer I told Clifford to interview,"

laughed Mr. Harmer. "It was John C. Keefe. I didn't know Reefer was in town, but even if I had I wouldn't have thought it a particle of use to send a man to him. He has never consented to be interviewed before on any known subject, and he's been especially close-mouthed about this bill, although men from all the big papers in the country have been after him. He is notorious on that score. Why, Patty, it's the biggest journalistic fish that has ever been landed in this office. Andrew Reefer's opinion on the bill will have a tremendous influence. We'll run the interview as a leader in a special edition that is under way already. Of course, he must have been ready to give the information to the public or nothing would have induced him to open his mouth. But to think that we should be the first to get it! Patty, you're a brick!"

Clifford came home on the seven o'clock train, and Patty was there to meet him, brimful of her story. But Clifford also had a story to tell and got his word in first.

"Now, Patty, don't scold until you hear why I missed the train. I met Mr. Peabody of the Steel and Iron Company at Mr. Moreland's and got into conversation with him. When he found out who I was, he was greatly interested and said Father had been one of his best friends when they were at college together. I told him about wanting to get the position in the company, and he had me go right out to the works and see about it. And, Patty, I have the place. Goodbye to the grind of newspaper items and fillers. I tried to get back to the station at Bancroft in time to catch the train but I couldn't, and it was just as well, for Mr. Keefe was suddenly summoned home this afternoon, and when the three-thirty train from town stopped at Bancroft he was on it. I found that out and I got on, going to the next station with him and getting my interview after all. It's here in my notebook, and I must hurry up to the office and hand it in. I suppose Mr. Harmer will be very much vexed until he finds that I have it."

"Oh, no. Mr. Harmer is in a very good humour," said Patty with dancing eyes. Then she told her story.

The interview with Mr. Reefer came out with glaring headlines, and the *Chronicle* had its hour of fame and glory. The next day Mr. Harmer sent word to Patty that he wanted to see her.

"So Clifford is leaving," he said abruptly when she entered the office. "Well, do you want his place?"

"Mr. Harmer, are you joking?" demanded Patty in amazement.

"Not I. That stuff you handed in was splendidly written—I didn't have to use the pencil more than once or twice. You have the proper journalist instinct all right. We need a lady on the staff anyhow, and if you'll take the place it's yours for saying so, and the permanency next month."

"I'll take it," said Patty promptly and joyfully.

"Good. Go down to the Symphony Club rehearsal this afternoon and report it. You've just ten minutes to get there," and Patty joyfully and promptly departed.

Aunt Caroline's Silk Dress

Patty came in from her walk to the post office with cheeks finely reddened by the crisp air. Carry surveyed her with pleasure. Of late Patty's cheeks had been entirely too pale to please Carry, and Patty had not had a very good appetite. Once or twice she had even complained of a headache. So Carry had sent her to the office for a walk that night, although the post office trip was usually Carry's own special constitutional, always very welcome to her after a weary day of sewing on other people's pretty dresses.

Carry never sewed on pretty dresses for herself, for the simple reason that she never had any pretty dresses. Carry was twenty-two—and feeling forty, her last pretty dress had been when she was a girl of twelve, before her father had died. To be sure, there was the silk organdie Aunt Kathleen had sent her, but that was fit only for parties, and Carry never went to any parties.

"Did you get any mail, Patty?" she asked unexpectantly. There was never much mail for the Lea girls.

"Yes'm," said Patty briskly. "Here's the *Weekly Advocate*, and a patent medicine almanac with all your dreams expounded, *and* a letter for Miss Carry M. Lea. It's postmarked Enfield, and has a suspiciously matrimonial look. I'm sure it's an invitation to Chris Fairley's wedding. Hurry up and see, Caddy."

Carry, with a little flush of excitement on her face, opened her letter. Sure enough, it contained an invitation "to be present at the marriage of Christine Fairley."

"How jolly!" exclaimed Patty. "Of course you'll go, Caddy. You'll have a chance to wear that lovely organdie of yours at last."

"It was sweet of Chris to invite me," said Carry. "I really didn't expect it."

"Well, I did. Wasn't she your most intimate friend when she lived in Enderby?"

"Oh, yes, but it is four years since she left, and some people might forget in four years. But I might have known Chris wouldn't. Of course I'll go."

"And you'll make up your organdie?"

"I shall have to," laughed Carry, forgetting all her troubles for a moment, and feeling young and joyous over the prospect of a festivity. "I haven't another thing that would do to wear to a wedding. If I hadn't that blessed organdie I couldn't go, that's all."

"But you have it, and it will look lovely made up with a tucked skirt. Tucks are so fashionable now. And there's that lace of mine you can have for a bertha. I want you to look just right, you see. Enfield is a big place, and there will be lots of grandees at the wedding. Let's get the last fashion sheet and pick out a design right away. Here's one on the very first page that would be nice. You could wear it to perfection, Caddy you're so tall and slender. It wouldn't suit a plump and podgy person like myself at all."

Carry liked the pattern, and they had an animated discussion over it. But, in the end, Carry sighed, and pushed the sheet away from her, with all the brightness gone out of face.

"It's no use, Patty. I'd forgotten for a few minutes, but it's all come back now. I can't think of weddings and new dresses, when the thought of that interest crowds everything else out. It's due next month—fifty dollars—and I've only ten saved up. I can't make forty dollars in a month, even if I had any amount of sewing, and you know hardly anyone wants sewing done just now. I don't know what we shall do. Oh, I suppose we can rent a couple of rooms in the village and *exist* in them. But it breaks my heart to think of leaving our old home."

"Perhaps Mr. Kerr will let us have more time," suggested Patty, not very hopefully. The sparkle had gone out of her face too. Patty loved their little home as much as Carry did.

"You know he won't. He has been only too anxious for an excuse to foreclose, this long time. He wants the land the house is on. Oh, if I only hadn't been sick so long in the summer—just when everybody had sewing to do. I've tried so hard to catch up, but I couldn't." Carry's voice broke in a sob.

Patty leaned over the table and patted her sister's glossy dark hair gently.

"You've worked too hard, dearie. You've just gone to skin and bone. Oh, I know how hard it is! I can't bear to think of leaving this dear old spot either. If we could only induce Mr. Kerr to give us a year's grace! I'd be teaching then, and we could easily pay the interest and some of the principal too. Perhaps he will if we both go to him and coax very hard. Anyway, don't worry over it till after the wedding. I want you to go and have a good time. You never have good times, Carry."

"Neither do you," said Carry rebelliously. "You never have anything that other girls have, Patty—not even pretty clothes."

"Deed, and I've lots of things to be thankful for," said Patty cheerily. "Don't you fret about me. I'm vain enough to think I've got some brains anyway, and I'm a-meaning to do something with them too. Now I think I'll go upstairs and study this evening. It will be warm enough there tonight, and the noise of the machine rather bothers me."

Patty whisked out, and Carry knew she should go to her sewing. But she sat a long while at the table in dismal thought. She was so tired, and so hopeless. It had been such a hard struggle, and it seemed now as if it would all come to naught. For five years, ever since her mother's death, Carry had supported herself and Patty by dressmaking. They had been a hard five years of pinching and economizing and going without, for Enderby was only a small place, and there were two other dressmakers. Then there was always the mortgage to devour everything. Carry had kept it at bay till now, but at last she was conquered. She had had typhoid fever in the spring and had not been able to work for a long time. Indeed, she had gone to work before she should. The doctor's bill was yet unpaid, but Dr. Hamilton had told her to take her time. Carry knew she would not be pressed for that, and next year Patty would be able to help her. But next year would be too late. The dear little home would be lost then.

When Carry roused herself from her sad reflections, she saw a crumpled note lying on the floor. She picked it up and absently smoothed it out. Seeing Patty's name at the top she was about to lay it aside without reading it, but the lines were few, and the sense of them flashed into Carry's brain. The note was an invitation to Clare Forbes's party! The Lea girls had known that the Forbes girls were going to give a party, but they had not expected that Patty would be invited. Of course, Clare Forbes was in Patty's class at school and was always very nice and friendly with her. But then the Forbes set was not the Lea set.

Carry ran upstairs to Patty's room. "Patty, you dropped this on the floor. I couldn't help seeing what it was. Why didn't you tell me Clare had invited you?"

"Because I knew I couldn't go, and I thought you would feel badly over that. Caddy, I wish you hadn't seen it."

"Oh, Patty, I *do* wish you could go to the party. It was so sweet of Clare to invite you, and perhaps she will be offended if you don't go—she won't understand. Clare Forbes isn't a girl whose friendship is to be lightly thrown away when it is offered."

"I know that. But, Caddy dear, it is impossible. I don't think that I have any foolish pride about clothes, but you know it is out of the question to think of going to Clare

Forbes's party in my last winter's plaid dress, which is a good two inches too short and skimpy in proportion. Putting my own feelings aside, it would be an insult to Clare. There, don't think any more about it."

But Carry did think about it. She lay awake half the night wondering if there might not be some way for Patty to go to that party. She knew it was impossible, unless Patty had a new dress, and how could a new dress be had? Yet she did so want Patty to go. Patty never had any good times, and she was studying so hard. Then, all at once, Carry thought of a way by which Patty might have a new dress. She had been tossing restlessly, but now she lay very still, staring with wide-open eyes at the moonlit window, with the big willow boughs branching darkly across it. Yes, it was a way, but could she? *Could* she? Yes, she could, and she would. Carry buried her face in her pillow with a sob and a gulp. But she had decided what must be done, and how it must be done.

"Are you going to begin on your organdie today?" asked Patty in the morning, before she started for school.

"I must finish Mrs. Pidgeon's suit first," Carry answered. "Next week will be time enough to think about my wedding garments."

She tried to laugh and failed. Patty thought with a pang that Carry looked horribly pale and tired—probably she had worried most of the night over the interest. "I'm so glad she's going to Chris's wedding," thought Patty, as she hurried down the street. "It will take her out of herself and give her something nice to think of for ever so long."

Nothing more was said that week about the organdie, or the wedding, or the Forbes's party. Carry sewed fiercely, and sat at her machine for hours after Patty had gone to bed. The night before the party she said to Patty, "Braid your hair tonight, Patty. You'll want it nice and wavy to go to the Forbes's tomorrow night."

Patty thought that Carry was actually trying to perpetrate a weak joke, and endeavoured to laugh. But it was a rather dreary laugh. Patty, after a hard evening's study, felt tired and discouraged, and she was really dreadfully disappointed about the party, although she wouldn't have let Carry suspect it for the world.

"You're going, you know," said Carry, as serious as a judge, although there was a little twinkle in her eyes.

"In a faded plaid two inches too short?" Patty smiled as brightly as possible.

"Oh, no. I have a dress all ready for you." Carry opened the wardrobe door and took out—the loveliest girlish dress of creamy organdie, with pale pink roses scattered over it, made with the daintiest of ruffles and tucks, with a bertha of soft creamy lace, and a girdle of white silk. "This is for you," said Carry.

Patty gazed at the dress with horror-stricken eyes. "Caroline Lea, *that is your organdie!* And you've gone and made it up for *me*! Carry Lea, what are you going to wear to the wedding?"

"Nothing. I'm not going."

"You are—you must—you shall. I won't take the organdie."

"You'll have to now, because it's made to fit you. Come, Patty dear, I've set my heart on your going to that party. You mustn't disappoint me—you *can't*, for what good would it do? I can never wear the dress now."

Patty realized that. She knew she might as well go to the party, but she did not feel much pleasure in the prospect. Nevertheless, when she was ready for it the next evening, she couldn't help a little thrill of delight. The dress was so pretty, and dainty, and becoming.

"You look sweet," exclaimed Carry admiringly. "There, I hear the Browns' carriage. Patty, I want you to promise me this—that you'll not let any thought of me, or my not going to the wedding, spoil your enjoyment this evening. I gave you the dress that you might have a good time, so don't make my gift of no effect."

"I'll try," promised Patty, flying downstairs, where her next-door neighbours were waiting for her.

At two o'clock that night Carry was awakened to see Patty bending over her, flushed and radiant. Carry sat sleepily up. "I hope you had a good time," she said.

"I had—oh, I had—but I didn't waken you out of your hard-earned slumbers at this wee sma' hour to tell you that. Carry, I've thought of a way for you to go to the wedding. It just came to me at supper. Mrs. Forbes was sitting opposite to me, and her dress suggested it. You must make over Aunt Caroline's silk dress."

"Nonsense," said Carry, a little crossly; even sweet-tempered people are sometimes cross when they are wakened up for—as it seemed—nothing.

"It's good plain sense. Of course, you must make it over and—"

"Patty Lea, you're crazy. I wouldn't dream of wearing that hideous thing. Bright green silk, with huge yellow brocade flowers as big as cabbages all over it! I think I see myself in it."

"Caddy, listen to me. You know there's enough of that black lace of mother's for the waist, and the big black lace shawl of Grandmother Lea's will do for the skirt. Make it over—"

"A plain slip of the silk," gasped Carry, her quick brain seizing on all the possibilities of the plan. "Why didn't I think of it before? It will be just the thing, the greens and yellow will be toned down to a nice shimmer under the black lace. And I'll make cuffs of black velvet with double puffs above—and just cut out a wee bit at the throat with a frill of lace and a band of black velvet ribbon around my neck. Patty Lea, it's an inspiration."

Carry was out of bed by daylight the next morning and, while Patty still slumbered, she mounted to the garret, and took Aunt Caroline's silk dress from the chest where it had lain forgotten for three years. Carry held it up at arm's length, and looked at it with amusement.

"It is certainly ugly, but with the lace over it it will look very different. There's enough of it, anyway, and that skirt is stiff enough to stand alone. Poor Aunt

Caroline, I'm afraid I wasn't particularly grateful for her gift at the time, but I really am now."

Aunt Caroline, who had given the dress to Carry three years before, was, an old lady of eighty, the aunt of Carry's father. She had once possessed a snug farm but in an evil hour she had been persuaded to deed it to her nephew, Edward Curry, whom she had brought up. Poor Aunt Caroline had lived to regret this step, for everyone in Enderby knew that Edward Curry and his wife had repaid her with ingratitude and greed.

Carry, who was named for her, was her favourite grandniece and often went to see her, though such visits were coldly received by the Currys, who always took especial care never to leave Aunt Caroline alone with any of her relatives. On one occasion, when Carry was there, Aunt Caroline had brought out this silk dress.

"I'm going to give this to you, Carry," she said timidly. "It's a good silk, and not so very old. Mr. Greenley gave it to me for a birthday present fifteen years ago. Maybe you can make it over for yourself."

Mrs. Edward, who was on duty at the time, sniffed disagreeably, but she said nothing. The dress was of no value in her eyes, for the pattern was so ugly and old-fashioned that none of her smart daughters would have worn it. Had it been otherwise, Aunt Caroline would probably not have been allowed to give it away.

Carry had thanked Aunt Caroline sincerely. If she did not care much for the silk, she at least prized the kindly motive behind the gift. Perhaps she and Patty laughed a little over it as they packed it away in the garret. It was so very ugly, but Carry thought it was sweet of Aunt Caroline to have given her something. Poor old Aunt Caroline had died soon after, and Carry had not thought about the silk dress again. She had too many other things to think of, this poor worried Carry.

After breakfast Carry began to rip the skirt breadths apart. Snip, snip, went her scissors, while her thoughts roamed far afield—now looking forward with renewed pleasure to Christine's wedding, now dwelling dolefully on the mortgage. Patty, who was washing the dishes, knew just what her thoughts were by the light and shadow on her expressive face.

"Why!—what?" exclaimed Carry suddenly. Patty wheeled about to see Carry staring at the silk dress like one bewitched. Between the silk and the lining which she had just ripped apart was a twenty-dollar bill, and beside it a sheet of letter paper covered with writing in a cramped angular hand, both secured very carefully to the silk.

"Carry Lea!" gasped Patty.

With trembling fingers Carry snipped away the stitches that held the letter, and read it aloud.

"My dear Caroline," it ran, "I do not know when you will find this letter and this money, but when you do it belongs to you. I have a hundred dollars which I always meant to give you because you were named for me. But Edward and his wife do not know I have it, and I don't want them to find out. They would not let me give it to you if they knew, so I have thought of this way of getting it to you. I have sewed five twenty-dollar bills under the lining of this skirt, and they are all yours, with your Aunt Caroline's best love. You were always a good girl, Carry, and you've worked hard, and I've given Edward enough. Just take this money and use it as you like.

"Aunt Caroline Greenley."

"Carry Lea, are we both dreaming?" gasped Patty.

With crimson cheeks Carry ripped the other breadths apart, and there were the other four bills. Then she slipped down in a little heap on the sofa cushions and began to cry—happy tears of relief and gladness.

"We can pay the interest," said Patty, dancing around the room, "and get yourself a nice new dress for the wedding."

"Indeed I won't," said Carry, sitting up and laughing through her tears. "I'll make over this dress and wear it out of gratitude to the memory of dear Aunt Caroline."

Aunt Susanna's Thanksgiving Dinner

"Here's Aunt Susanna, girls," said Laura who was sitting by the north window—nothing but north light does for Laura who is the artist of our talented family.

Each of us has a little pet new-fledged talent which we are faithfully cultivating in the hope that it will amount to something and soar highly some day. But it is difficult to cultivate four talents on our tiny income. If Laura wasn't such a good manager we never could do it.

Laura's words were a signal for Kate to hang up her violin and for me to push my pen and portfolio out of sight. Laura had hidden her brushes and water colors as she spoke. Only Margaret continued to bend serenely over her Latin grammar. Aunt Susanna frowns on musical and literary and artistic ambitions but she accords a faint approval to Margaret's desire for an education. A college course, with a tangible diploma at the end, and a sensible pedagogic aspiration is something Aunt Susanna can understand when she tries hard. But she cannot understand messing with paints, fiddling, or scribbling, and she has only unmeasured contempt for messers, fiddlers, and scribblers. Time was when we had paid no attention to Aunt Susanna's views on these points; but ever since she had, on one incautious day when she was in high good humor, dropped a pale, anemic little hint that she might send Margaret to college if she were a good girl we had been bending all our energies towards securing Aunt Susanna's approval. It was not enough that Aunt Susanna should approve of Margaret; she must approve of the whole four of us or she would not help Margaret. That is Aunt Susanna's way. Of late we had been growing a little discouraged. Aunt Susanna had recently read a magazine article which stated that the higher education of women was ruining our country and that a woman who was a B.A. couldn't, in the very nature of things, ever be a housewifely, cookly creature. Consequently, Margaret's chances looked a little foggy; but we hadn't quite given up hope. A very little thing might sway Aunt Susanna one way or the other, so that we walked very softly and tried to mingle serpents' wisdom and doves' harmlessness in practical portions.

When Aunt Susanna came in Laura was crocheting, Kate was sewing, and I was poring over a recipe book. That was not deception at all, since we did all these things frequently—much more frequently, in fact, than we painted or fiddled or wrote. But Aunt Susanna would never believe it. Nor did she believe it now.

She threw back her lovely new sealskin cape, looked around the sitting-room and then smiled—a truly Aunt Susannian smile.

"What a pity you forgot to wipe that smudge of paint off your nose, Laura," she said sarcastically. "You don't seem to get on very fast with your lace. How long is it since you began it? Over three months, isn't it?"

"This is the third piece of the same pattern I've done in three months, Aunt Susanna," said Laura presently. Laura is an old duck. She never gets cross and snaps back. I do; and it's so hard not to with Aunt Susanna sometimes. But I generally manage it for I'd do anything for Margaret. Laura did not tell Aunt Susanna that she sold her lace at the Women's Exchange in town and made enough to buy her new hats. She makes enough out of her water colors to dress herself.

Aunt Susanna took a second breath and started in again.

"I notice your violin hasn't quite as much dust on it as the rest of the things in this room, Kate. It's a pity you stopped playing just as I came in. I don't enjoy fiddling much but I'd prefer it to seeing anyone using a needle who isn't accustomed to it."

Kate is really a most dainty needlewoman and does all the fine sewing in our family. She colored and said nothing—that being the highest pitch of virtue to which our Katie, like myself, can attain.

"And there's Margaret ruining her eyes over books," went on Aunt Susanna severely. "Will you kindly tell me, Margaret Thorne, what good you ever expect Latin to do you?"

"Well, you see, Aunt Susanna," said Margaret gently—Magsie and Laura are birds of a feather—"I want to be a teacher if I can manage to get through, and I shall need Latin for that."

All the girls except me had now got their accustomed rap, but I knew better than to hope I should escape.

"So you're reading a recipe book, Agnes? Well, that's better than poring over a novel. I'm afraid you haven't been at it very long though. People generally don't read recipes upside down—and besides, you didn't quite cover up your portfolio. I see a corner of it sticking out. Was genius burning before I came in? It's too bad if I quenched the flame."

"A cookery book isn't such a novelty to me as you seem to think, Aunt Susanna," I said, as meekly as it was possible for me. "Why I'm a real good cook—'if I do say it as hadn't orter.'"

I am, too.

"Well, I'm glad to hear it," said Aunt Susanna skeptically, "because that has to do with my errand her to-day. I'm in a peck of troubles. Firstly, Miranda Mary's mother has had to go and get sick and Miranda Mary must go home to wait on her. Secondly, I've just had a telegram from my sister-in-law who has been ordered west for her health, and I'll have to leave on to-night's train to see her before she goes. I can't get back until the noon train Thursday, and that is Thanksgiving, and I've invited Mr. and Mrs. Gilbert to dinner that day. They'll come on the same train. I'm dreadfully worried. There doesn't seem to be anything I can do except get on of you girls to go up to the Pinery Thursday morning and cook the dinner for us. Do you think you can manage it?"

We all felt rather dismayed, and nobody volunteered with a rush. But as I had just boasted that I could cook it was plainly my duty to step into the breach, and I did it with fear and trembling.

"I'll go, Aunt Susanna," I said.

"And I'll help you," said Kate.

"Well, I suppose I'll have to try you," said Aunt Susanna with the air of a woman determined to make the best of a bad business. "Here is the key of the kitchen door. You'll find everything in the pantry, turkey and all. The mince pies are all ready made so you'll only have to warm them up. I want dinner sharp at twelve for the train is due at 11:50. Mr. and Mrs. Gilbert are very particular and I do hope you will have things right. Oh, if I could only be home myself! Why will people get sick at such inconvenient times?"

"Don't worry, Aunt Susanna," I said comfortingly. "Kate and I will have your Thanksgiving dinner ready for you in tiptop style."

"Well I'm sure I hope so. Don't get to mooning over a story, Agnes. I'll lock the library up and fortunately there are no fiddles at the Pinery. Above all, don't let any of the McGinnises in. They'll be sure to be prowling around when I'm not home. Don't give that dog of theirs any scraps either. That is Miranda Mary's one fault. She will feed that dog in spite of all I can do and I can't walk out of my own back door without falling over him."

We promise to eschew the McGinnises and all their works, including the dog, and when Aunt Susanna had gone we looked at each other with mingled hope and fear.

"Girls, this is the chance of your lives," said Laura. "If you can only please Aunt Susanna with this dinner it will convince her that you are good cooks in spite of your nefarious bent for music and literature. I consider the illness of Miranda Mary's mother a Providential interposition—that is, if she isn't too sick."

"It's all very well for you to be pleased, Lolla," I said dolefully. "But I don't feel jubilant over the prospect at all. Something will probably go wrong. And then there's our own nice little Thanksgiving celebration we've planned, and pinched and economized for weeks to provide. That is half spoiled now."

"Oh, what is that compared to Margaret's chance of going to college?" exclaimed Kate. "Cheer up, Aggie. You know we can cook. I feel that it is now or never with Aunt Susanna."

I cheered up accordingly. We are not given to pessimism which is fortunate. Ever since father died four years ago we have struggled on here, content to give up a good deal just to keep our home and be together. This little gray house—oh, how we do love it and its apple trees—is ours and we have, as aforesaid, a tiny income and our ambitions; not very big ambitions but big enough to give zest to our lives and hope to the future. We've been very happy as a rule. Aunt Susanna has a big house and lots of money but she isn't as happy as we are. She nags us a good deal—just as she used to nag father—but we don't mind it very much after all. Indeed, I sometimes suspect that we really like Aunt Susanna tremendously if she'd only leave us alone long enough to find it out.

Thursday morning was an ideal Thanksgiving morning—bright, crisp and sparkling. There had been a white frost in the night, and the orchard and the white birch wood behind it looked like fairyland. We were all up early. None of us had slept well, and both Kate and I had had the most fearful dreams of spoiling Aunt Susanna's Thanksgiving dinner.

"Never mind, dreams always go by contraries, you know," said Laura cheerfully. "You'd better go up to the Pinery early and get the fires on, for the house will be cold. Remember the McGinnises and the dog. Weigh the turkey so that you'll know exactly how long to cook it. Put the pies in the oven in time to get piping hot— lukewarm mince pies are an abomination. Be sure—"

"Laura, don't confuse us with any more cautions," I

groaned, "or we shall get hopelessly fuddled. Come on, Kate, before she has time to."

It wasn't very far up to the Pinery—just ten minutes' walk, and such a delightful walk on that delightful morning. We went through the orchard and then through the white birch wood where the loveliness of the frosted boughs awed us. Beyond that there was a lane between ranks of young, balsamy, white-misted firs and then an open pasture field, sere and crispy. Just across it was the Pinery, a lovely old house with dormer windows in the roof, surrounded by pines that were dark and glorious against the silvery morning sky.

The McGinnis dog was sitting on the back-door steps when we arrived. He wagged his tail ingratiatingly, but we ruthlessly pushed him off, went in and shut the door in his face. All the little McGinnises were sitting in a row on their fence, and they whooped derisively. The McGinnis manners are not those which appertain to the caste of Vere de Vere; but we rather like the urchins—there are eight of them—and we would probably have gone over to talk to them if we had not had the fear of Aunt Susanna before our eyes.

We kindled the fires, weighed the turkey, put it in the oven and prepared the vegetables. Then we set the dining-room table and decorated it with Aunt Susanna's potted ferns and dishes of lovely red apples. Everything went so smoothly that we soon forgot to be nervous. When the turkey was done, we took it out, set it on the back of the range to keep warm and put the mince pies in. The potatoes, cabbage and turnips were bubbling away cheerfully, and everything was going as merrily as a marriage bell. Then, all at once, things happened.

In an evil hour we went to the yard window and looked out. We saw a quiet scene. The McGinnis dog was still sitting on his haunches by the steps, just as he had been sitting all the morning. Down in the McGinnis yard everything wore an unusually peaceful aspect. Only one McGinnis was in sight—Tony, aged eight, who was perched up on the edge of the well box, swinging his legs and singing at the top of his melodious Irish voice. All at once, just as we were looking at him, Tony went over backward and apparently tumbled head foremost down his father's well.

Kate and I screamed simultaneously. We tore across the kitchen, flung open the door, plunged down over Aunt Susanna's yard, scrambled over the fence and flew to the well. Just as we reached it, Tony's red head appeared as he climbed serenely out over the box. I don't know whether I felt more relieved or furious. He had merely fallen on the blank guard inside the box: and there are times when I am tempted to think he fell on purpose because he saw Kate and me looking out at the window. At least he didn't seem at all frightened, and grinned most impishly at us.

Kate and I turned on our heels and marched back in as dignified a manner as was possible under the circumstances. Half way up Aunt Susanna's yard we forgot dignity and broke into a run. We had left the door open and the McGinnis dog had disappeared.

Never shall I forget the sight we saw or the smell we smelled when we burst into that kitchen. There on the floor was the McGinnis dog and what was left of Aunt Susanna's Thanksgiving turkey. As for the smell, imagine a commingled odor of scorching turnips and burning mince pies, and you have it.

The dog fled out with a guilty yelp. I groaned and snatched the turnips off. Kate threw open the oven door and dragged out the pies. Pies and turnips were ruined as irretrievably as the turkey.

"Oh, what shall we do?" I cried miserably. I knew Margaret's chance of college was gone forever.

"Do!" Kate was superb. She didn't lose her wits for a second. "We'll go home and borrow the girls' dinner. Quick—there's just ten minutes before train time. Throw those pies and turnips into this basket—the turkey too— we'll carry them with us to hide them."

I might not be able to evolve an idea like that on the spur of the moment, but I can at least act up to it when it is presented. Without a moment's delay we shut the door and ran. As we went I saw the McGinnis dog licking his chops over in their yard. I have been ashamed ever since of my feelings toward that dog. They were murderous. Fortunately I had no time to indulge them.

It is ten minutes walk from the Pinery to our house, but you can run it in five. Kate and I burst into the kitchen just as Laura and Margaret were sitting down to dinner. We had neither time nor breath for explanations. Without a word I grasped the turkey platter and the turnip tureen. Kate caught one hot mince pie from the oven and whisked a cold one out of the pantry.

"We've—got—to have—them," was all she said.

I've always said that Laura and Magsie would rise to any occasion. They saw us carry their Thanksgiving dinner off under their very eyes and they never interfered by word or motion. They didn't even worry us with questions. They realized that something desperate had happened and that the emergency called for deed not words.

"Aggie," gasped Kate behind me as we tore through the birch wood, "the border—of these pies—is crimped—differently—from Aunt Susanna's."

"She—won't know—the difference," I panted. "Miranda—Mary—crimps them."

We got back to the Pinery just as the train whistle blew. We had ten minutes to transfer turkey and turnips to Aunt Susanna's dishes, hide our own, air the kitchen, and get back our breath. We accomplished it. When Aunt Susanna and her guests came we were prepared for them: we were calm—outwardly—and the second mince pie was getting hot in the oven. It was ready by the time it was needed. Fortunately our turkey was the same size as Aunt Susanna's, and Laura had cooked a double supply of turnips, intending to warm them up the next day. Still, all things considered, Kate and I didn't enjoy that dinner much. We kept thinking of poor Laura and Magsie at home, dining off potatoes on Thanksgiving!

But at least Aunt Susanna was satisfied. When Kate

and I were washing the dishes she came out quite beamingly.

"Well, my dears, I must admit that you made a very good job of the dinner, indeed. The turkey was done to perfection. As for the mince pies—well, of course Miranda Mary made them, but she must have had extra good luck with them, for they were excellent and heated to just the right degree. You didn't give anything to the McGinnis dog, I hope?"

"No, we didn't give him anything," said Kate.

Aunt Susanna did not notice the emphasis.

When we had finished the dishes we smuggled our platter and tureen out of the house and went home. Laura and Margaret were busy painting and studying and were just as sweet-tempered as if we hadn't robbed them of their dinner. But we had to tell them the whole story before we even took off our hats.

"There is a special Providence for children and idiots," said Laura gently. We didn't ask her whether she meant us or Tony McGinnis or both. There are some things better left in obscurity. I'd have probably said something much sharper than that if anybody had made off with my Thanksgiving turkey so unceremoniously.

Aunt Susanna came down the next day and told Margaret that she would send her to college. Also she commissioned Laura to paint her a water-color for her dining-room and said she'd pay her five dollars for it.

Kate and I were rather left out in the cold in this distribution of favors, but when you come to reflect that Laura and Magsie had really cooked that dinner, it was only just.

Anyway, Aunt Susanna has never since insinuated that we can't cook, and that is as much as we deserve.

Fair Exchange and No Robbery

Katherine Rangely was packing up. Her chum and roommate, Edith Wilmer, was sitting on the bed watching her in that calm disinterested fashion peculiarly maddening to a bewildered packer.

"It does seem too provoking," said Katherine, as she tugged at an obstinate shawl strap, "that Ned should be transferred here now, just when I'm going away. The powers that be might have waited until vacation was over. Ned won't know a soul here and he'll be horribly lonesome."

"I'll do my best to befriend him, with your permission," said Edith consolingly.

"Oh, I know. You're a special Providence, Ede. Ned will be up tonight first thing, of course, and I'll introduce him. Try to keep the poor fellow amused until I get back. Two months! Just fancy! And Aunt Elizabeth won't abate one jot or tittle of the time I promised to stay with her. Harbour Hill is so frightfully dull, too."

Then the talk drifted around to Edith's affairs. She was engaged to a certain Sidney Keith, who was a professor in some college.

"I don't expect to see much of Sidney this summer," said Edith. "He's writing another book. He is so terribly addicted to literature."

"How lovely," sighed Katherine, who had aspirations in that line herself. "If only Ned were like him I should be perfectly happy. But Ned is so prosaic. He doesn't care a rap for poetry, and he laughs when I enthuse. It makes him quite furious when I talk of taking up writing seriously. He says women writers are an abomination on the face of the earth. Did you ever hear anything so ridiculous?"

"He is very handsome, though," said Edith, with a glance at his photograph on Katherine's dressing table. "And that is what Sid is not. He is rather distinguished looking, but as plain as he can possibly be."

Edith sighed. She had a weakness for handsome men and thought it rather hard that fate should have allotted her so plain a lover.

"He has lovely eyes," said Katherine comfortingly, "and handsome men are always vain. Even Ned is. I have to snub him regularly. But I think you'll like him."

Edith thought so too when Ned Ellison appeared that night. He was a handsome off-handed young fellow, who seemed to admire Katherine immensely, and be a little afraid of her into the bargain.

"Edith will try to make Riverton pleasant for you while I am away," she told him in their good-bye chat. "She is a dear girl—you'll like her, I know. It's really too bad I have to go away now, but it can't be helped."

"I shall be awfully lonesome," grumbled Ned. "Don't you forget to write regularly, Kitty."

"Of course I'll write, but for pity's sake, Ned, don't call me Kitty. It sounds so childish. Well, bye-bye, dear boy. I'll be back in two months and then we'll have a lovely time."

* * *

When Katherine had been at Harbour Hill for a week she wondered how upon earth she was going to put in the remaining seven. Harbour Hill was noted for its beauty, but not every woman can live by scenery alone.

"Aunt Elizabeth," said Katherine one day, "does anybody ever die in Harbour Hill? Because it doesn't seem to me it would be any change for them if they did."

Aunt Elizabeth's only reply to this was a shocked look.

To pass the time Katherine took to collecting

seaweeds, and this involved long tramps along the shore. On one of these occasions she met with an adventure. The place was a remote spot far up the shore. Katherine had taken off her shoes and stockings, tucked up her skirt, rolled her sleeves high above her dimpled elbows, and was deep in the absorbing process of fishing up seaweeds off a craggy headland. She looked anything but dignified while so employed, but under the circumstances dignity did not matter.

Presently she heard a shout from the shore and, turning around in dismay, she beheld a man on the rocks behind her. He was evidently shouting at her. What on earth could the creature want?

"Come in," he called, gesticulating wildly. "You'll be in the bottomless pit in another moment if you don't look out."

"He certainly must be a lunatic," said Katherine to herself, "or else he's drunk. What am I to do?"

"Come in, I tell you," insisted the stranger. "What in the world do you mean by wading out to such a place? Why, it's madness."

Katherine's indignation got the better of her fear.

"I do not think I am trespassing," she called back as icily as possible.

The stranger did not seem to be snubbed at all. He came down to the very edge of the rocks where Katherine could see him plainly. He was dressed in a somewhat well-worn grey suit and wore spectacles. He did not look like a lunatic, and he did not seem to be drunk.

"I implore you to come in," he said earnestly. "You must be standing on the very brink of the bottomless pit."

He is certainly off his balance, thought Katherine. He must be some revivalist who has gone insane on one point. I suppose I'd better go in. He looks quite capable of wading out here after me if I don't.

She picked her steps carefully back with her precious specimens. The stranger eyed her severely as she stepped on the rocks.

"I should think you would have more sense than to

risk your life in that fashion for a handful of seaweeds," he said.

"I haven't the faintest idea what you mean," said Miss Rangely. "You don't look crazy, but you talk as if you were."

"Do you mean to say you don't know that what the people hereabouts call the Bottomless Pit is situated right off that point—the most dangerous spot along the whole coast?"

"No, I didn't," said Katherine, horrified. She remembered now that Aunt Elizabeth had warned her to be careful of some bad hole along shore, but she had not been paying much attention and had supposed it to be in quite another direction. "I am a stranger here."

"Well, I hardly thought you'd be foolish enough to be out there if you knew," said the other in mollified accents. "The place ought not to be left without warning, anyhow. It is the most careless thing I ever heard of. There is a big hole right off that point and nobody has ever been able to find the bottom of it. A person who got into it would never be heard of again. The rocks there form an eddy that sucks everything right down."

"I am very grateful to you for calling me in," said Katherine humbly. "I had no idea I was in such danger."

"You have a very fine bunch of seaweeds, I see," said the unknown.

But Katherine was in no mood to converse on seaweeds. She suddenly realized what she must look like—bare feet, draggled skirts, dripping arms. And this creature whom she had taken for a lunatic was undoubtedly a gentleman. Oh, if he would only go and give her a chance to put on her shoes and stockings!

Nothing seemed further from his intentions. When Katherine had picked up the aforesaid articles and turned homeward, he walked beside her, still discoursing on seaweeds as eloquently as if he were commonly accustomed to walking with barefooted young women. In spite of herself, Katherine couldn't help listening to him, for he managed to invest seaweeds with an absorbing interest. She finally decided that as he didn't seem to mind her bare feet, she wouldn't either.

He knew so much about seaweeds that Katherine felt decidedly amateurish beside him. He looked over her specimens and pointed out the valuable ones. He explained the best method of preserving and mounting them, and told her of other and less dangerous places along the shore where she might get some new varieties.

When they came in sight of Harbour Hill, Katherine began to wonder what on earth she would do with him. It wasn't exactly permissible to snub a man who had practically saved your life, but, on the other hand, the prospect of walking through the principal street of Harbour Hill barefooted and escorted by a scholarly looking gentleman discoursing on seaweeds was not to be calmly contemplated.

The unknown cut the Gordian knot himself. He said that he must really go back or he would be late for dinner, lifted his hat politely, and departed. Katherine waited until he was out of sight, then sat down on the sand and put on her shoes and stockings.

"Who on earth can he be?" she said to herself. "And where have I seen him before? There was certainly something familiar about his appearance. He is very nice, but he must have thought me crazy. I wonder if he belongs to Harbour Hill."

The mystery was solved when she got home and found a letter from Edith awaiting her.

"I see Ned quite often," wrote the latter, "and I think he is perfectly splendid. You are a lucky girl, Kate. But oh, do you know that Sidney is actually at Harbour Hill, too, or at least quite near it? I had a letter from him yesterday. He has gone down there to spend his vacation, because it is so quiet, and to finish up some horrid scientific book he is working at. He's boarding at some little farmhouse up the shore. I've written to him today to hunt you up and consider himself introduced to you. I think you'll like him, for he's just your style."

Katherine smiled when Sidney Keith's card was

brought up to her that evening and went down to meet him. Her companion of the morning rose to meet her.

"You!" he said.

"Yes, me," said Miss Rangely cheerfully and ungrammatically. "You didn't expect it, did you? I was sure I had seen you before—only it wasn't you but your photograph."

When Professor Keith went away it was with a cordial invitation to call again. He did not fail to avail himself of it—in fact, he became a constant visitor at Sycamore Villa. Katherine wrote all about it to Edith and cultivated Professor Keith with a clear conscience.

They got on capitally together. They went on long expeditions up shore after seaweeds, and when seaweeds were exhausted they began to make a collection of the Harbour Hill flora. This involved more long, companionable expeditions. Katherine sometimes wondered when Professor Keith found time to work on his book, but as he made no reference to the subject, neither did she.

Once in a while, when she had time to think of them, she wondered how Ned and Edith were getting on. At first Edith's letters had been full of Ned, but in her last two or three she had said little about him. Katherine wrote and jokingly asked Edith if she and Ned had quarreled. Edith wrote back and said, "What nonsense." She and Ned were as good friends as ever, but he was getting acquainted in Riverton now and wasn't so dependent on her society, etc.

Katherine sighed and went on a fern hunt with Professor Keith. It was getting near the end of her vacation and she had only two weeks more. They were sitting down to rest on the side of the road when she mentioned this fact inconsequently. The professor prodded the harmless dust with his cane. Well, he supposed she would find a return to work pleasant and would doubtless be glad to see her Riverton friends again.

"I'm dying to see Edith," said Katherine.

"And Ned?" suggested Professor Keith.

"Oh yes. Ned, of course," assented Katherine without

enthusiasm. There didn't seem to be anything more to say. One cannot talk everlastingly about ferns, so they got up and went home.

Katherine wrote a particularly affectionate letter to Ned that night. Then she went to bed and cried.

When Professor Keith came up to bid Miss Rangely good-bye on the eve of her departure from Harbour Hill, he looked like a man who was being led to execution without benefit of clergy. But he kept himself well in hand and talked calmly on impersonal subjects. After all, it was Katherine who made the first break when she got up to say good-bye. She was in the middle of some conventional sentence when she suddenly stopped short, and her voice trailed off in a babyish quiver.

The professor put out his arm and drew her close to him. His hat dropped under their feet and was trampled on, but I doubt if Professor Keith knows the difference to this day, for he was fully absorbed in kissing Katherine's hair. When she became cognizant of this fact, she drew herself away.

"Oh, Sidney, don't!—think of Edith! I feel like a traitor."

"Do you think she would care very much if I—if you—if we—" hesitated the professor.

"Oh, it would break her heart," cried Katherine with convincing earnestness. "I know it would—and Ned's too. They must never know."

The professor stooped and began hunting for his maltreated hat. He was a long time finding it, and when he did he went softly to the door. With his hand on the knob, he paused and looked back.

"Good-bye, Miss Rangely," he said softly.

But Katherine, whose face was buried in the cushions of the lounge, did not hear him and when she looked up he was gone.

* * *

Katharine felt that life was stale, flat and unprofitable when she alighted at Riverton station in the dusk of the next evening. She was not expected until a later train and there was no one to meet her. She walked drearily through the streets to her boarding house and entered her room unannounced. Edith, who was lying on the bed, sprang up with a surprised greeting. It was too dark to be sure, but Katherine had an uncomfortable suspicion that her friend had been crying, and her heart quaked guiltily. Could Edith have suspected anything?

"Why, we didn't think you'd be up till the 8:30 train, and Ned and I were going to meet you."

"I found I could catch an earlier train, so I took it," said Katherine, as she dropped listlessly into a chair. "I am tired to death and I have such a headache. I can't see anyone tonight, not even Ned."

"You poor dear," said Edith sympathetically, beginning a search for the cologne. "Lie down on the bed and I'll bathe your poor head. Did you have a good time at Harbour Hill? And how did you leave Sid? Did he say anything about coming up?"

"Oh, he was quite well," said Katherine wearily. "I didn't hear him say if he intended to come up or not. There, thanks—that will do nicely."

After Edith had gone down, Katherine tossed about restlessly. She knew Ned had come and she did not want to see him. But, after all, it was only putting off the evil day, and it was treating him rather shabbily. She would go down for a minute.

There were two doors to the parlour, and Katherine went by way of the library one, over which a portiere was hanging. Her hand was lifted to draw it back when she heard something that arrested the movement.

A woman was crying in the room beyond. It was Edith—and what was she saying?

"Oh, Ned, it is all perfectly dreadful! I couldn't look Catherine in the face when she came home. I'm so ashamed of myself and I never meant to be so false. We must never let her suspect for a minute."

"It's pretty rough on a fellow," said another voice—

Ned's voice—in a choked sort of a way. "Upon my word, Edith, I don't see how I'm going to keep it up."

"You must," sobbed Edith. "It would break her heart—and Sidney's too. We must just make up our minds to forget each other, Ned, and you must marry Katherine."

Just at this point Katherine became aware that she was eavesdropping and she went away noiselessly. She did not look in the least like a person who has received a mortal blow, and she had forgotten her headache altogether.

When Edith came up half an hour later, she found the worn-out invalid sitting up and reading a novel.

"How is your headache, dear?" she asked, carefully keeping her face turned away from Katherine.

"Oh, it's all gone," said Miss Rangely cheerfully.

"Why didn't you come down then? Ned was here."

"Well, Ede, I did go down, but I thought I wasn't particularly wanted, so I came back."

Edith faced her friend in dismay, forgetful of swollen lids and tear-stained cheeks.

"Katherine!"

"Don't look so conscience stricken, my dear child. There is no harm done."

"You heard—"

"Some surprising speeches. So you and Ned have gone and fallen in love with one another?"

"Oh, Katherine," sobbed Edith, "we—we—couldn't help it—but it's all over. Oh, don't be angry with me!"

"Angry? My dear, I'm delighted."

"Delighted?"

"Yes, you dear goose. Can't you guess, or must I tell you? Sidney and I did the very same, and had just such a melancholy parting last night as I suspect you and Ned had tonight."

"Katherine!"

"Yes, it's quite true. And of course we made up our minds to sacrifice ourselves on the altar of duty and all that. But now, thank goodness, there is no need of such wholesale immolation. So just let's forgive each other."

"Oh," sighed Edith happily, "it is almost too good to be true."

"It is really providentially ordered, isn't it?" said Katherine. "Ned and I would never have got on together in the world, and you and Sidney would have bored each other to death. As it is, there will be four perfectly happy people instead of four miserable ones. I'll tell Ned so tomorrow."

Anna's Love Letters

"Are you going to answer Gilbert's letter tonight, Anna?" asked Alma Williams, standing in the pantry doorway, tall, fair, and grey-eyed, with the sunset light coming down over the dark firs, through the window behind her, and making a primrose nimbus around her shapely head.

Anna, dark, vivid, and slender, was perched on the edge of the table, idly swinging her slippered foot at the cat's head. She smiled wickedly at Alma before replying.

"I am not going to answer it tonight or any other night," she said, twisting her full, red lips in a way that Alma had learned to dread. Mischief was ripening in Anna's brain when that twist was out.

"What do you mean?" asked Alma anxiously.

"Just what I say, dear," responded Anna, with deceptive meekness. "Poor Gilbert is gone, and I don't intend to bother my head about him any longer. He was amusing while he lasted, but of what use is a beau two thousand miles away, Alma?"

Alma was patient—outwardly. It was never of any avail to show impatience with Anna.

"Anna, you are talking foolishly. Of course you are going to answer his letter. You are as good as engaged to him. Wasn't that practically understood when he left?"

"No, no, dear," and Anna shook her sleek black head with the air of explaining matters to an obtuse child. "*I* was the only one who understood. Gil *mis*understood. He thought that I would really wait for him until he should have made enough money to come home and pay off the mortgage. I let him think so, because I hated to

134

hurt his little feelings. But now it's off with the old love and on with a new one for me."

"Anna, you cannot be in earnest!" exclaimed Alma.

But she was afraid that Anna was in earnest. Anna had a wretched habit of being in earnest when she said flippant things.

"You don't mean that you are not going to write to Gilbert at all—after all you promised?"

Anna placed her elbows daintily on the top of the rocking chair, dropped her pointed chin in her hands, and looked at Alma with black demure eyes.

"I—do—mean—just—that," she said slowly. "I never mean to marry Gilbert Murray. This is final, Alma, and you need not scold or coax, because it would be a waste of breath. Gilbert is safely out of the way, and now I am going to have a good time with a few other delightful men creatures in Exeter."

Anna nodded decisively, flashed a smile at Alma, picked up her cat, and went out. At the door she turned and looked back, with the big black cat snuggled under her chin.

"If you think Gilbert will feel very badly over his letter not being answered, you might answer it yourself, Alma," she said teasingly. "There it is"—she took the letter from the pocket of her ruffled apron and threw it on a chair. "You may read it if you want to; it isn't really a love letter. I told Gilbert he wasn't to write silly letters. Come, pussy, I'm going to get ready for prayer meeting. We've got a nice, new, young, good-looking minister in Exeter, pussy, and that makes prayer meeting *very* interesting."

Anna shut the door, her departing laugh rippling mockingly through the dusk. Alma picked up Gilbert Murray's letter and went to her room. She wanted to cry, since she could not shake Anna. Even if she could have shook her, it would only have made her more perverse. Anna was in earnest; Alma knew that, even while she hoped and believed that it was but the earnestness of a freak that would pass in time. Anna had had one like it a year ago, when she had cast Gilbert off for three months, driving him distracted by flirting with Charlie Moore. Then she had suddenly repented and taken him back. Alma thought that this whim would run its course likewise and leave a repentant Anna. But meanwhile everything might be spoiled. Gilbert might not prove forgiving a second time.

Alma would have given much if she could only have induced Anna to answer Gilbert's letter, but coaxing Anna to do anything was a very sure and effective way of preventing her from doing it.

* * *

Alma and Anna had lived alone at the old Williams homestead ever since their mother's death four years before. Exeter matrons thought this hardly proper, since Alma, in spite of her grave ways, was only twenty-four. The farm was rented, so that Alma's only responsibilities were the post office which she kept, and that harum-scarum beauty of an Anna.

The Murray homestead adjoined theirs. Gilbert Murray had grown up with Alma; they had been friends ever since she could remember. Alma loved Gilbert with a love which she herself believed to be purely sisterly, and which nobody else doubted could be, since she had been at pains to make a match—Exeter matrons' phrasing—between Gil and Anna, and was manifestly delighted when Gilbert obligingly fell in love with the latter.

There was a small mortgage on the Murray place which Mr. Murray senior had not been able to pay off. Gilbert determined to get rid of it, and his thoughts turned to the west. His father was an active, hale old man, quite capable of managing the farm in Gilbert's absence. Alexander MacNair had gone to the west two years previously and got work on a new railroad. He wrote to Gilbert to come too, promising him plenty of work and good pay. Gilbert went, but before going he had asked Anna to marry him.

It was the first proposal Anna had ever had, and she managed it quite cleverly, from her standpoint. She told Gilbert that he must wait until he came home again before settling that, meanwhile, they would be *very* good friends—emphasized with a blush—and that he might write to her. She kissed him goodbye, and Gilbert, honest fellow, was quite satisfied. When an Exeter girl had allowed so much to be inferred, it was understood to be equivalent to an engagement. Gilbert had never discerned that Anna was not like the other Exeter girls, but was a law unto herself.

Alma sat down by her window and looked out over the lane where the slim wild cherry trees were bronzing under the autumn frosts. Her lips were very firmly set. Something must be done. But what?

Alma's heart was set on this marriage for two reasons. Firstly, if Anna married Gilbert she would be near her all her life. She could not bear the thought that some day Anna might leave her and go far away to live. In the second and largest place, she desired the marriage because Gilbert did. She had always been desirous, even in the old, childish play-days, that Gilbert should get just exactly what he wanted. She had always taken a keen, strange delight in furthering his wishes.

Anna's falseness would surely break his heart, and Alma winced at the thought of his pain.

There was one thing she could do. Anna's tormenting suggestion had fallen on fertile soil. Alma balanced pros and cons, admitting the risk. But she would have taken a tenfold larger risk in the hope of holding secure Anna's place in Gilbert's affections until Anna herself should come to her senses.

When it grew quite dark and Anna had gone lilting down the lane on her way to prayer meeting, Alma lighted her lamp, read Gilbert's letter—and answered it. Her handwriting was much like Anna's. She signed the letter "A. Williams," and there was nothing in it that might not have been written by her to Gilbert; but she knew that Gilbert would believe Anna had written it, and she intended him so to believe. Alma never did a thing halfway when she did it at all. At first she wrote rather constrainedly but, reflecting that in any case Anna would have written a merely friendly letter, she allowed her thoughts to run freely, and the resulting epistle was an excellent one of its kind. Alma had the gift of expression and more brains than Exeter people had ever imagined she possessed. When Gilbert read that letter a fortnight later he was surprised to find that Anna was so clever. He had always, with a secret regret, thought her much inferior to Alma in this respect, but that delightful letter, witty, wise, fanciful, was the letter of a clever woman.

When a year had passed Alma was still writing to Gilbert the letters signed "A. Williams." She had ceased to fear being found out, and she took a strange pleasure in the correspondence for its own sake. At first she had been quakingly afraid of discovery. When she smuggled the letters addressed in Gilbert's handwriting to Miss Anna Williams out of the letter packet and hid them from Anna's eyes, she felt as guilty as if she were breaking all the laws of the land at once. To be sure, she knew that she would have to confess to Anna some day, when the latter repented and began to wish she had written to Gilbert, but that was a very different thing from premature disclosure.

But Anna had as yet given no sign of such repentance, although Alma looked for it anxiously. Anna was having the time of her life. She was the acknowledged beauty of five settlements, and she went forward on her career of conquest quite undisturbed by the jealousies and heart-burnings she provoked on every side.

One moonlight night she went for a sleigh-drive with Charlie Moore of East Exeter—and returned to tell Alma that they were married!

"I knew you would make a fuss, Alma, because you don't like Charlie, so we just took matters into our own hands. It was so much more romantic, too. I'd always said I'd never be married in any of your dull, commonplace ways. You might as well forgive me and be nice right off, Alma, because you'd have to do it anyway, in time. Well, you do look surprised!"

* * *

Alma accepted the situation with an apathy that amazed Anna. The truth was that Alma was stunned by a thought that had come to her even while Anna was speaking.

"Gilbert will find out about the letters now, and despise me."

Nothing else, not even the fact that Anna had married shiftless Charlie Moore, seemed worth while considering beside this. The fear and shame of it haunted her like a nightmare; she shrank every morning from the thought of all the mail that was coming that day, fearing that there would be an angry, puzzled letter from Gilbert. He must certainly soon hear of Anna's marriage; he would see it in the home paper, other correspondents in Exeter would write him of it. Alma grew sick at heart thinking of the complications in front of her.

When Gilbert's letter came she left it for a whole day before she could summon courage to open it. But it was a harmless epistle after all; he had not yet heard of Anna's marriage. Alma had at first no thought of answering it, yet her fingers ached to do so. Now that Anna was gone, her loneliness was unbearable. She realized how much Gilbert's letters had meant to her, even when written to another woman. She could bear her life well enough, she thought, if she only had his letters to look forward to.

No more letters came from Gilbert for six weeks. Then came one, alarmed at Anna's silence, anxiously asking the reason for it; Gilbert had heard no word of the marriage. He was working in a remote district where newspapers seldom penetrated. He had no other correspondent in Exeter now; except his mother, and she, not knowing that he supposed himself engaged to Anna had forgotten to mention it.

Alma answered that letter. She told herself recklessly that she would keep on writing to him until he found out. She would lose his friendship anyhow, when that occurred, but meanwhile she would have the letters a little longer. She could not learn to live without them until she had to.

The correspondence slipped back into its old groove. The harassed look which Alma's face had worn, and which Exeter people had attributed to worry over Anna, disappeared. She did not even feel lonely, and reproached herself for lack of proper feeling in missing Anna so little. Besides, to her horror and dismay, she detected in herself a strange undercurrent of relief at the thought that Gilbert could never marry Anna now! She could not understand it. Had not that marriage been her dearest wish for years? Why then should she feel this strange gladness at the impossibility of its fulfilment? Altogether, Alma feared that her condition of mind and morals must be sadly askew. Perhaps, she thought mournfully, this perversion of proper feeling was her punishment for the deception she had practised. She had deliberately done evil that good might come, and now the very imaginations of her heart were stained by that evil. Alma cried herself to sleep many a night in her repentance, but she kept on writing to Gilbert, for all that.

The winter passed, and the spring and summer waned, and Alma's outward life flowed as smoothly as the currents of the seasons, broken only by vivid eruptions from Anna, who came over often from East Exeter, glorying in her young matronhood, "to cheer Alma up." Alma, so said Exeter people, was becoming unsociable and old maidish. She lost her liking for company, and seldom went anywhere among her neighbours. Her once frequent visits across the yard to chat with old Mrs. Murray became few and far between. She could not bear to hear the old lady talking about Gilbert, and she was afraid that some day she would be told that he was coming home. Gilbert's home-coming was the nightmare dread that darkened poor Alma's whole horizon.

* * *

One October day, two years after Gilbert's departure, Alma, standing at her window in the reflected glow of a red maple outside, looked down the lane and saw him striding up it! She had had no warning of his coming. His last letter, dated three weeks back, had not hinted at it. Yet there he was—and with him Alma's Nemesis.

She was very calm. Now that the worst had come, she felt quite strong to meet it. She would tell Gilbert the truth, and he would go away in anger and never forgive her, but she deserved it. As she went downstairs, the only thing that really worried her was the thought of the pain Gilbert would suffer when she told him of Anna's faithlessness. She had seen his face as he passed under her window, and it was the face of a blithe man who had not heard any evil tidings. It was left to her to tell him; surely, she thought apathetically, that was punishment enough for what she had done.

With her hand on the doorknob, she paused to wonder what she should say when he asked her why she had not told him of Anna's marriage when it occurred—why she had still continued the deception when it had no longer an end to serve. Well, she would tell him the truth—that it was because she could not bear the thought of giving up writing to him. It was a humiliating thing to confess, but that did not matter—nothing mattered now. She opened the door.

Gilbert was standing on the big round door-stone under the red maple—a tall, handsome young fellow with a bronzed face and laughing eyes. His exile had improved him. Alma found time and ability to reflect that she had never known Gilbert was so fine-looking.

He put his arm around her and kissed her cheek in his frank delight at seeing her again. Alma coldly asked him in. Her face was still as pale as when she came downstairs, but a curious little spot of fiery red blossomed out where Gilbert's lips had touched it.

Gilbert followed her into the sitting-room and looked about eagerly.

"When did you come home?" she said slowly. "I did not know you were expected."

"Got homesick, and just came! I wanted to surprise

you all," he answered, laughing. "I arrived only a few minutes ago. Just took time to hug my mother, and here I am. Where's Anna?"

The pent-up retribution of two years descended on Alma's head in the last question of Gilbert's. But she did not flinch. She stood straight before him, tall and fair and pale, with the red maple light streaming in through the open door behind her, staining her light house-dress and mellowing the golden sheen of her hair. Gilbert reflected that Alma Williams was really a very handsome girl. These two years had improved her. What splendid big grey eyes she had! He had always wished that Anna's eyes had not been quite so black.

"Anna is not here," said Alma. "She is married."

"Married!"

Gilbert sat down suddenly on a chair and looked at Alma in bewilderment.

"She has been married for a year," said Alma steadily. "She married Charlie Moore of East Exeter, and has been living there ever since."

"Then," said Gilbert, laying hold of the one solid fact that loomed out of the mist of his confused understanding, "why did she keep on writing letters to me after she was married?"

"She never wrote to you at all. It was I that wrote the letters."

Gilbert looked at Alma doubtfully. Was she crazy? There was something odd about her, now that he noticed, as she stood rigidly there, with that queer red spot on her face, a strange fire in her eyes, and that weird reflection from the maple enveloping her like an immaterial flame.

"I don't understand," he said helplessly.

Still standing there, Alma told the whole story, giving full explanations, but no excuses. She told it clearly and simply, for she had often pictured this scene to herself and thought out what she must say. Her memory worked automatically, and her tongue obeyed it promptly. To herself she seemed like a machine, talking mechanically, while her soul stood on one side and listened.

When she had finished there was a silence lasting perhaps ten seconds. To Alma it seemed like hours. Would Gilbert overwhelm her with angry reproaches, or would he simply rise up and leave her in unutterable contempt? It was the most tragic moment of her life, and her whole personality was strung up to meet it and withstand it.

"Well, they were good letters, anyhow," said Gilbert finally; "interesting letters," he added, as if by way of a meditative afterthought.

It was so anti-climactic that Alma broke into an hysterical giggle, cut short by a sob. She dropped into a chair by the table and flung her hands over her face, laughing and sobbing softly to herself. Gilbert rose and walked to the door, where he stood with his back to her until she regained her self-control. Then he turned and looked down at her quizzically.

Alma's hands lay limply in her lap, and her eyes were cast down, with tears glistening on the long fair lashes. She felt his gaze on her.

"Can you ever forgive me, Gilbert?" she said humbly.

"I don't know that there is much to forgive," he answered. "I have some explanations to make too and, since we're at it, we might as well get them all over and have done with them. Two years ago I did honestly think I was in love with Anna—at least when I was round where she was. She had a taking way with her. But, somehow, even then, when I wasn't with her she seemed to kind of grow dim and not count for so awful much after all. I used to wish she was more like you—quieter, you know, and not so sparkling. When I parted from her that last night before I went west, I did feel very bad, and she seemed very dear to me, but it was six weeks from that before her—your—letter came, and in that time she seemed to have faded out of my thoughts. Honestly, I wasn't thinking much about her at all. Then came the letter—and it was a splendid one, too. I had never thought that Anna could write a letter like that, and I was as pleased as Punch about it. The letters kept coming, and I kept on looking for them more and more all the time. I fell in love all over again—with the writer of those letters. I thought it was Anna, but since you wrote the letters, it must have been with you, Alma. I thought it was because she was growing more womanly that she could write such letters. That was why I came home. I wanted to get acquainted all over again, before she grew beyond me altogether—I wanted to find the real Anna the letters showed me. I—I—didn't expect this. But I don't care if Anna is married, so long as the girl who wrote those letters isn't. It's you I love, Alma."

He bent down and put his arm about her, laying his cheek against hers. The little red spot where his kiss had fallen was now quite drowned out in the colour that rushed over her face.

"If you'll marry me, Alma, I'll forgive you," he said.

A little smile escaped from the duress of Alma's lips and twitched her dimples.

"I'm willing to do anything that will win your forgiveness, Gilbert," she said meekly.

The Girl Who Drove the Cows

"I wonder who that pleasant-looking girl who drives cows down the beech lane every morning and evening is," said Pauline Palmer, at the tea table of the country farmhouse where she and her aunt were spending the summer. Mrs. Wallace had wanted to go to some fashionable watering place, but her husband had bluntly told her he couldn't afford it. Stay in the city when all her set were out she would not, and the aforesaid farmhouse had been the compromise.

"I shouldn't suppose it could make any difference to you who she is," said Mrs. Wallace impatiently. "I do wish, Pauline, that you were more careful in your choice of associates. You hobnob with everyone, even that old man who comes around buying eggs. It is very bad form."

Pauline hid a rather undutiful smile behind her napkin. Aunt Olivia's snobbish opinions always amused her.

"You've no idea what an interesting old man he is," she said. "He can talk more entertainingly than any other man I know. What is the use of being so exclusive, Aunt Olivia? You miss so much fun. You wouldn't be so horribly bored as you are if you fraternized a little with the 'natives,' as you call them."

"No, thank you," said Mrs. Wallace disdainfully.

"Well, I am going to try to get acquainted with that girl," said Pauline resolutely. "She looks nice and jolly."

"I don't know where you get your low tastes from," groaned Mrs. Wallace. "I'm sure it wasn't from your poor mother. What do you suppose the Morgan Knowles would think if they saw you taking up with some tomboy girl on a farm?"

"I don't see why it should make a great deal of difference what they would think, since they don't seem to be aware of my existence, or even of yours, Aunty," said Pauline, with twinkling eyes. She knew it was her aunt's dearest desire to get in with the Morgan Knowles' "set"—a desire that seemed as far from being realized as ever. Mrs. Wallace could never understand why the Morgan Knowles shut her from their charmed circle. They certainly associated with people much poorer and of more doubtful worldly station than hers—the Markhams, for instance, who lived on an unfashionable street and wore quite shabby clothes. Just before she had left Colchester, Mrs. Wallace had seen Mrs. Knowles and Mrs. Markham together in the former's automobile. James Wallace and Morgan Knowles were associated in business dealings; but in spite of Mrs. Wallace's schemings and aspirations and heart burnings, the association remained a purely business one and never advanced an inch in the direction of friendship.

As for Pauline, she was hopelessly devoid of social ambitions and she did not in the least mind the Morgan Knowles' remote attitude.

"Besides," continued Pauline, "she isn't a tomboy at all. She looks like a very womanly, well-bred sort of girl. Why should you think her a tomboy because she drives cows? Cows are placid, useful animals—witness this delicious cream which I am pouring over my blueberries. And they have to be driven. It's an honest occupation."

"I daresay she is someone's servant," said Mrs. Wallace contemptuously. "But I suppose even that wouldn't matter to you, Pauline?"

"Not a mite," said Pauline cheerfully. "One of the very nicest girls I ever knew was a maid Mother had the last year of her dear life. I loved that girl, Aunt Olivia, and I correspond with her. She writes letters that are ten times more clever and entertaining than those stupid epistles Clarisse Gray sends me—and Clarisse Gray is a rich man's daughter and is being educated in Paris."

"You are incorrigible, Pauline," said Mrs. Wallace hopelessly.

"Mrs. Boyd," said Pauline to their landlady, who now made her appearance, "who is that girl who drives the cows along the beech lane mornings and evenings?"

"Ada Cameron, I guess," was Mrs. Boyd's response. "She lives with the Embrees down on the old Embree place just below here. They're pasturing their cows on the upper farm this summer. Mrs. Embree is her father's half-sister."

"Is she as nice as she looks?"

"Yes, Ada's a real nice sensible girl," said Mrs. Boyd. "There is no nonsense about her."

"That doesn't sound very encouraging," murmured Pauline, as Mrs. Boyd went out. "I like people with a little nonsense about them. But I hope better things of Ada, Mrs. Boyd to the contrary notwithstanding. She has a pair of grey eyes that can't possibly always look sensible. I think they must mellow occasionally into fun and jollity and wholesome nonsense. Well, I'm off to the shore. I want to get that photograph of the Cove this evening, if possible. I've set my heart on taking first prize at the Amateur Photographers' Exhibition this fall, and if I can only get that Cove with all its beautiful lights and shadows, it will be the gem of my collection."

Pauline, on her return from the shore, reached the beech lane just as the Embree cows were swinging down it. Behind them came a tall, brown-haired, brown-faced girl in a neat print dress. Her hat was hung over her arm, and the low evening sunlight shone redly over her smooth glossy head. She carried herself with a pretty dignity, but when her eyes met Pauline's, she looked as if she would smile on the slightest provocation.

Pauline promptly gave her the provocation.

"Good evening, Miss Cameron," she called blithely. "Won't you please stop a few moments and look me over? I want to see if you think me a likely person for a summer chum."

Ada Cameron did more than smile. She laughed outright and went over to the fence where Pauline was sitting on a stump. She looked down into the merry black eyes of the town girl she had been half envying for a week and said humorously: "Yes, I think you very likely, indeed. But it takes two to make a friendship—like a bargain. If I'm one, you'll have to be the other."

"I'm the other. Shake," said Pauline, holding out her hand.

That was the beginning of a friendship that made poor Mrs. Wallace groan outwardly as well as inwardly. Pauline and Ada found that they liked each other even more than they had expected to. They walked, rowed, berried and picnicked together. Ada did not go to Mrs. Boyd's a great deal, for some instinct told her that Mrs. Wallace did not look favourably on her, but Pauline spent half her time at the little, brown, orchard-embowered house at the end of the beech lane where the Embrees lived. She had never met any girl she thought so nice as Ada.

"She is nice every way," she told the unconvinced Aunt Olivia. "She's clever and well read. She is sensible and frank. She has a sense of humour and a great deal of insight into character—witness her liking for your niece! She can talk interestingly and she can also be silent when silence is becoming. And she has the finest profile I ever saw. Aunt Olivia, may I ask her to visit me next winter?"

"No, indeed," said Mrs. Wallace, with crushing emphasis. "You surely don't expect to continue this absurd intimacy past the summer, Pauline?"

"I expect to be Ada's friend all my life," said Pauline laughingly, but with a little ring of purpose in her voice. "Oh, Aunty, dear, can't you see that Ada is just the same girl in cotton print that she would be in silk attire? She is really far more distinguished looking than any girl in the Knowles' set."

"Pauline!" said Aunt Olivia, looking as shocked as if Pauline had committed blasphemy.

Pauline laughed again, but she sighed as she went to her room. Aunt Olivia has the kindest heart in the world, she thought. What a pity she isn't able to see things as they really are! My friendship with Ada can't be perfect if I can't invite her to my home. And she is such a dear girl—the first real friend after my own heart that I've ever had.

The summer waned, and August burned itself out.

"I suppose you will be going back to town next week? I shall miss you dreadfully," said Ada.

The two girls were in the Embree garden, where Pauline was preparing to take a photograph of Ada standing among the asters, with a great sheaf of them in her arms. Pauline wished she could have said: But you must come and visit me in the winter. Since she could not, she had to content herself with saying: "You won't miss me any more than I shall miss you. But we'll correspond, and I hope Aunt Olivia will come to Marwood again next summer."

"I don't think I shall be here then," said Ada with a sigh. "You see, it is time I was doing something for myself, Pauline. Aunt Jane and Uncle Robert have always been very kind to me, but they have a large family and are not very well off. So I think I'll try for a situation in one of the Remington stores this fall."

"It's such a pity you couldn't have gone to the Academy and studied for a teacher's licence," said Pauline, who knew what Ada's ambitions were.

"I should have liked that better, of course," said Ada quietly. "But it is not possible, so I must do my best at the next best thing. Don't let's talk of it. It might make me feel blueish and I want to look especially pleasant if I'm going to have my photo taken."

"You couldn't look anything else," laughed Pauline. "Don't smile too broadly—I want you to be looking over the asters with a bit of a dream on your face and in your eyes. If the picture turns out as beautiful as I fondly expect, I mean to put it in my exhibition collection under the title 'A September Dream.' There, that's the very expression. When you look like that, you remind me of somebody I have seen, but I can't remember who it is. All ready now—don't move—there, dearie, it is all over."

When Pauline went back to Colchester, she was busy for a month preparing her photographs for the exhibition, while Aunt Olivia renewed her spinning of all the little social webs in which she fondly hoped to entangle the Morgan Knowles and other desirable flies.

When the exhibition was opened, Pauline Palmer's collection won first prize, and the prettiest picture in it was one called "A September Dream"—a tall girl with a wistful face, standing in an old-fashioned garden with her arms full of asters.

The very day after the exhibition was opened the Morgan Knowles' automobile stopped at the Wallace door. Mrs. Wallace was out, but it was Pauline whom stately Mrs. Morgan Knowles asked for. Pauline was at that moment buried in her darkroom developing photographs, and she ran down just as she was—a fact which would have mortified Mrs. Wallace exceedingly if she had ever known it. But Mrs. Morgan Knowles did not seem to mind at all. She liked Pauline's simplicity of manner. It was more than she had expected from the aunt's rather vulgar affectations.

"I have called to ask you who the original of the photograph 'A September Dream' in your exhibit was, Miss Palmer," she said graciously. "The resemblance to a very dear childhood friend of mine is so startling that I am sure it cannot be accidental."

"That is a photograph of Ada Cameron, a friend whom I met this summer up in Marwood," said Pauline.

"Ada Cameron! She must be Ada Frame's daughter, then," exclaimed Mrs. Knowles in excitement. Then, seeing Pauline's puzzled face, she explained: "Years ago, when I was a child, I always spent my summers on the farm of my uncle, John Frame. My cousin, Ada Frame, was the dearest friend I ever had, but after we grew up we saw nothing of each other, for I went with my parents to Europe for several years, and Ada married a neighbour's son, Alec Cameron, and went out west. Her father, who was my only living relative other than my parents, died, and I never heard anything more of Ada until about eight years ago, when somebody told me she was dead and had left no family. That part of the report cannot have been true if this girl is her daughter."

"I believe she is," said Pauline quickly. "Ada was born out west and lived there until she was eight years old, when her parents died and she was sent east to her father's half-sister. And Ada looks like you—she always reminded me of somebody I had seen, but I never could decide who it was before. Oh, I hope it is true, for Ada is such a sweet girl, Mrs. Knowles."

"She couldn't be anything else if she is Ada Frame's daughter," said Mrs. Knowles. "My husband will investigate the matter at once, and if this girl is Ada's child we shall hope to find a daughter in her, as we have none of our own."

"What will Aunt Olivia say!" said Pauline with wickedly dancing eyes when Mrs. Knowles had gone.

Aunt Olivia was too much overcome to say anything. That good lady felt rather foolish when it was proved that the girl she had so despised was Mrs. Morgan Knowles' cousin and was going to be adopted by her. But to hear Aunt Olivia talk now, you would suppose that she and not Pauline had discovered Ada.

The latter sought Pauline out as soon as she came to Colchester, and the summer friendship proved a life-long one and was, for the Wallaces, the open sesame to the enchanted ground of the Knowles' "set."

"So everybody concerned is happy," said Pauline. "Ada is going to college and so am I, and Aunt Olivia is on the same committee as Mrs. Knowles for the big church bazaar. What about my 'low tastes' now, Aunt Olivia?"

"Well, who would ever have supposed that a girl who drove cows to pasture was connected with the Morgan Knowles?" said poor Aunt Olivia piteously.

The Revolt of Mary Isabel

"For a woman of forty, Mary Isabel, you have the least sense of any person I have ever known," said Louisa Irving.

Louisa had said something similar in spirit to Mary Isabel almost every day of her life. Mary Isabel had never resented it, even when it hurt her bitterly. Everybody in Latimer knew that Louisa Irving ruled her meek little sister with a rod of iron and wondered why Mary Isabel never rebelled. It simply never occurred to Mary Isabel to do so; all her life she had given in to Louisa and the thought of refusing obedience to her sister's Mede-and-Persian decrees never crossed her mind. Mary Isabel had only one secret from Louisa and she lived in daily dread that Louisa would discover it. It was a very harmless little secret, but Mary Isabel felt rightly sure that Louisa would not tolerate it for a moment.

They were sitting together in the dim living room of their quaint old cottage down by the shore. The window was open and the sea-breeze blew in, stirring the prim white curtains fitfully, and ruffling the little rings of dark hair on Mary Isabel's forehead—rings which always annoyed Louisa. She thought Mary Isabel ought to brush them straight back, and Mary Isabel did so faithfully a dozen times a day; and in ten minutes they crept down again, kinking defiance to Louisa, who might make Mary Isabel submit to her in all things but had no power over naturally curly hair. Louisa had never had any trouble with her own hair; it was straight and sleek and mouse-coloured—what there was of it.

Mary Isabel's face was flushed and her wood-brown eyes looked grieved and pleading. Mary Isabel was still pretty, and vanity is the last thing to desert a properly constructed woman.

"I can't wear a bonnet yet, Louisa," she protested. "Bonnets have gone out for everybody except really old ladies. I want a hat: one of those pretty, floppy ones with pale blue forget-me-nots."

Then it was that Louisa made the remark quoted above.

"I wore a bonnet before I was forty," she went on ruthlessly, "and so should every decent woman. It is absurd to be thinking so much of dress at your age, Mary Isabel. I don't know what sort of a way you'd bedizen yourself out if I'd let you, I'm sure. It's fortunate you have somebody to keep you from making a fool of yourself. I'm going to town tomorrow and I'll pick you out a suitable black bonnet. You'd look nice starring round in leghorn and forget-me-nots, now, wouldn't you?"

Mary Isabel privately thought she would, but she gave in, of course, although she did hate bitterly that unbought, unescapable bonnet.

"Well, do as you think best, Louisa," she said with a sigh. "I suppose it doesn't matter much. Nobody cares how I look anyhow. But can't I go to town with you? I want to pick out my new silk."

"I'm as good a judge of black silk as you," said Louisa shortly. "It isn't safe to leave the house alone."

"But I don't want a black silk," cried Mary Isabel. "I've worn black so long; both my silk dresses have been black. I want a pretty silver-grey, something like Mrs. Chester Ford's."

"Did anyone ever hear such nonsense?" Louisa wanted to know, in genuine amazement. "Silver-grey silk is the most unserviceable thing in the world. There's nothing like black for wear and real elegance. No, no, Mary Isabel, don't be foolish. You must let me choose for you; you know you never had any judgment.

Mother told you so often enough. Now, get your sunbonnet and take a walk to the shore. You look tired. I'll get the tea."

Louisa's tone was kind though firm. She Was really good to Mary Isabel as long as Mary Isabel gave her her own way peaceably. But if she had known Mary Isabel's secret she would never have permitted those walks to the shore.

Mary Isabel sighed again, yielded, and went out. Across a green field from the Irving cottage Dr. Donald Hamilton's big house was hooding itself in the shadows of the thick fir grove that enabled the doctor to have a garden. There was no shelter at the cottage, so the Irving "girls" never tried to have a garden. Soon after Dr. Hamilton had come there to live he had sent a bouquet of early daffodils over by his housekeeper. Louisa had taken them gingerly in her extreme fingertips, carried them across the field to the lawn fence, and cast them over it, under the amused grey eyes of portly Dr. Hamilton, who was looking out of his office window. Then Louisa had come back to the porch door and ostentatiously washed her hands.

"I guess that will settle Donald Hamilton," she told the secretly sorry Mary Isabel triumphantly, and it did settle him—at least as far as any farther social advances were concerned.

Dr. Hamilton was an excellent physician and an equally excellent man. Louisa Irving could not have picked a flaw in his history or character. Indeed, against Dr. Hamilton himself she had no grudge, but he was the brother of a man she hated and whose relatives were consequently taboo in Louisa's eyes. Not that the brother was a bad man either; he had simply taken the opposite side to the Irvings in a notable church feud of a dozen years ago, and Louisa had never since held any intercourse with him or his fellow sinners.

Mary Isabel did not look at the Hamilton house. She kept her head resolutely turned away as she went down the shore lane with its wild sweet loneliness of salt-withered grasses and piping sea-winds. Only when she turned the corner of the fir-wood, which shut her out from view of the houses, did she look timidly over the line-fence. Dr. Hamilton was standing there, where the fence ran out to the sandy shingle, smoking his little black pipe, which he took out and put away when Mary Isabel came around the firs. Men did things like that instinctively in Mary Isabel's company. There was something so delicately virginal about her, in spite of her forty years, that they gave her the reverence they would have paid to a very young, pure girl.

Dr. Hamilton smiled at the little troubled face under the big sunbonnet. Mary Isabel had to wear a sunbonnet. She would never have done it from choice.

"What is the matter?" asked the doctor, in his big, breezy, old-bachelor voice. He had another voice for sick-beds and rooms of bereavement, but this one suited best with the purring of the waves and winds.

"How do you know that anything is the matter?" Mary Isabel parried demurely.

"By your face. Come now, tell me what it is."

"It is really nothing. I have just been foolish, that is all. I wanted a hat with forget-me-nots and a grey silk, and Louisa says I must have black and a bonnet."

The doctor looked indignant but held his peace. He and Mary Isabel had tacitly agreed never to discuss Louisa, because such discussion would not make for harmony. Mary Isabel's conscience would not let the doctor say anything uncomplimentary of Louisa, and the doctor's conscience would not let him say anything complimentary. So they left her out of the question and talked about the sea and the boats and poetry and flowers and similar non-combustible subjects.

* * *

These clandestine meetings had been going on for two months, ever since the day they had just happened to meet below the firs. It never occurred to Mary Isabel that the doctor meant anything but friendship; and if it had occurred to the doctor, he did not think there would be much use in saying so. Mary Isabel was too hopelessly under Louisa's thumb. She might keep tryst below the firs occasionally—so long as Louisa didn't know—but to no farther lengths would she dare go. Besides, the doctor wasn't quite sure that he really wanted anything more. Mary Isabel was a sweet little woman, but Dr. Hamilton had been a bachelor so long that it would be very difficult for him to get out of the habit; so difficult that it was hardly worth while trying when such an obstacle as Louisa Irving's tyranny loomed in the way. So he never tried to make love to Mary Isabel, though he probably would have if he had thought it of any use. This does not sound very romantic, of course, but when a man is fifty, romance, while it may be present in the fruit, is assuredly absent in blossom.

"I suppose you won't be going to the induction of my nephew Thursday week?" said the doctor in the course of the conversation.

"No. Louisa will not permit it. I had hoped," said Mary Isabel with a sigh, as she braided some silvery shore-grasses nervously together, "that when old Mr. Moody went away she would go back to the church here. And I think she would if—if—"

"If Jim hadn't come in Mr. Moody's place," finished the doctor with his jolly laugh.

Mary Isabel coloured prettily. "It is not because he is your nephew, doctor. It is because—because—"

"Because he is the nephew of my brother who was on the other side in that ancient church fracas? Bless you, I understand. What a good hater your sister is! Such a tenacity in holding bitterness from one generation to another commands admiration of a certain sort. As for Jim, he's a nice little chap, and he is coming to live with me until the manse is repaired."

"I am sure you will find that pleasant," said Mary Isabel primly.

She wondered if the young minister's advent would

make any difference in regard to these shore-meetings; then decided quickly that it would not; then more quickly still that it wouldn't matter if it did.

"He will be company," admitted the doctor, who liked company and found the shore road rather lonesome. "I had a letter from him today saying that he'd come home with me from the induction. By the way, they're tearing down the old post office today. And that reminds me—by Jove, I'd all but forgotten. I promised to go up and see Mollie Marr this evening; Mollie's nerves are on the rampage again. I must rush."

With a wave of his hand the doctor hurried off. Mary Isabel lingered for some time longer, leaning against the fence, looking dreamily out to sea. The doctor was a very pleasant companion. If only Louisa would allow neighbourliness! Mary Isabel felt a faint, impotent resentment. She had never had anything other girls had: friends, dresses, beaus, and it was all Louisa's fault— Louisa who was going to make her wear a bonnet for the rest of her life. The more Mary Isabel thought of that bonnet the more she hated it.

That evening Warren Marr rode down to the shore cottage on horseback and handed Mary Isabel a letter; a strange, scrumpled, soiled, yellow letter. When Mary Isabel saw the handwriting on the envelope she trembled and turned as deadly pale as if she had seen a ghost:

"Here's a letter for you," said Warren, grinning. "It's been a long time on the way—nigh fifteen years. Guess the news'll be rather stale. We found it behind the old partition when we tore it down today."

"It is my brother Tom's writing," said Mary Isabel faintly. She went into the room trembling, holding the letter tightly in her clasped hands. Louisa had gone up to the village on an errand; Mary Isabel almost wished she were home; she hardly felt equal to the task of opening Tom's letter alone. Tom had been dead for ten years and this letter gave her an uncanny sensation; as of a message from the spirit-land.

Fifteen years, ago Thomas Irving had gone to

California and five years later he had died there. Mary Isabel, who had idolized her brother, almost grieved herself to death at the time.

Finally she opened the letter with ice-cold fingers. It had been written soon after Tom reached California. The first two pages were filled with descriptions of the country and his "job."

On the third Tom began abruptly:

Look here, Mary Isabel, you are not to let Louisa boss you about as she was doing when I was at home. I was going to speak to you about it before I came away, but I forgot. Lou is a fine girl, but she is too domineering, and the more you give in to her the worse it makes her. You're far too easy-going for your own welfare, Mary Isabel, and for your own sake I Wish you had more spunk. Don't let Louisa live your life for you; just you live it yourself. Never mind if there is some friction at first; Lou will give in when she finds she has to, and you'll both be the better for it, I want you to be real happy, Mary Isabel, but you won't be if you don't assert your independence. Giving in the way you do is bad for both you and Louisa. It will make her a tyrant and you a poor-spirited creature of no account in the world. Just brace up and stand firm.

When she had read the letter through Mary Isabel took it to her own room and locked it in her bureau drawer. Then she sat by her window, looking out into a sea-sunset, and thought it over. Coming in the strange way it had, the letter seemed a message from the dead, and Mary Isabel had a superstitious conviction that she must obey it. She had always had a great respect for Tom's opinion. He was right—oh, she felt that he was right. What a pity she had not received the letter long ago, before the shackles of habit had become so firmly riveted. But it was not too late yet. She would rebel at last and—how had Tom phrased it—oh, yes, assert her independence. She owed it to Tom; It had been his wish—and he was dead—and she would do her best to fulfil it.

"I shan't get a bonnet," thought Mary Isabel determinedly. "Tom wouldn't have liked me in a bonnet. From this out I'm just going to do exactly as Tom would have liked me to do, no matter how afraid I am of Louisa. And, oh, I am horribly afraid of her."

Mary Isabel was every whit as much afraid the next morning after breakfast but she did not look it, by reason of the flush on her cheeks and the glint in her brown eyes. She had put Tom's letter in the bosom of her dress and she pressed her fingertips on it that the crackle might give her courage.

"Louisa," she said firmly, "I am going to town with you."

"Nonsense," said Louisa shortly.

"You may call it nonsense if you like, but I am going," said Mary Isabel unquailingly. "I have made up my mind on that point, Louisa, and nothing you can say will alter it."

Louisa looked amazed. Never before had Mary Isabel set her decrees at naught.

"Are you crazy, Mary Isabel?" she demanded.

"No, I am not crazy. But I am going to town and I am going to get a silver-grey silk for myself and a new hat. I will not wear a bonnet and you need never mention it to me again, Louisa."

"If you are going to town I shall stay home," said Louisa in a cold, ominous tone that almost made Mary Isabel quake. If it had not been for that reassuring crackle of Tom's letter I fear Mary Isabel would have given in. "This house can't be left alone. If you go, I'll stay."

Louisa honestly thought that would bring the rebel to terms. Mary Isabel had never gone to town alone in her life. Louisa did not believe she would dare to go. But Mary Isabel did not quail. Defiance was not so hard after all, once you had begun.

Mary Isabel went to town and she went alone. She spent the whole delightful day in the shops, unhampered by Louisa's scorn and criticism in her examination of all the pretty things displayed. She selected a hat she felt sure Tom would like—a pretty crumpled grey straw with forget-me-nots and ribbons. Then she bought a grey silk of a lovely silvery shade.

When she got back home she unwrapped her packages and showed her purchases to Louisa. But Louisa neither looked at them nor spoke to Mary Isabel. Mary Isabel tossed her head and went to her own room. Her draught of freedom had stimulated her, and she did not mind Louisa's attitude half as much as she would have expected. She read Tom's letter over again to fortify herself and then she dressed her hair in a fashion she had seen that day in town and pulled out all the little curls on her forehead.

The next day she took the silver-grey silk to the Latimer dressmaker and picked out a fashionable design for it. When the silk dress came home, Louisa, who had thawed out somewhat in the meantime, unbent sufficiently to remark that it fitted very well.

"I am going to wear it to the induction tomorrow," Mary Isabel said, boldly to all appearances, quakingly in reality. She knew that she was throwing down the gauntlet for good and all. If she could assert and maintain her independence in this matter Louisa's power would be broken forever.

* * *

Twelve years before this, the previously mentioned schism had broken out in the Latimer church. The minister had sided with the faction which Louisa Irving opposed. She had promptly ceased going to his church and withdrew all financial support. She paid to the Marwood church, fifteen miles away, and occasionally she hired a team and drove over there to service. But she never entered the Latimer church again nor allowed Mary Isabel to do so. For that matter, Mary Isabel did not wish to go. She had resented the minister's attitude almost as bitterly as Louisa. But when Mr. Moody accepted a call elsewhere Mary Isabel hoped that she and Louisa might return to their old church home. Possibly they might have done so had not the congregation called the young, newly fledged James Anderson. Mary Isabel would not have cared for this, but Louisa sternly said that neither she nor any of hers should ever darken the doors of a church where the nephew of Martin Hamilton preached. Mary Isabel had regretfully acquiesced at the time, but now she had made up her mind to go to church and she meant to begin with the induction service.

Louisa stared at her sister incredulously.

"Have you taken complete leave of your senses, Mary Isabel?"

"No. I've just come to them," retorted Mary Isabel recklessly, gripping a chair-back desperately so that Louisa should not see how she was trembling. "It is all foolishness to keep away from church just because of an old grudge. I'm tired of staying home Sundays or driving fifteen miles to Marwood to hear poor old Mr. Grattan. Everybody says Mr. Anderson is a splendid young man and an excellent preacher, and I'm going to attend his services regularly."

Louisa had taken Mary Isabel's first defiance in icy disdain. Now she lost her temper and raged. The storm of angry words beat on Mary Isabel like hail, but she fronted it staunchly. She seemed to hear Tom's voice saying, "Live your own life, Mary Isabel; don't let Louisa live it for you," and she meant to obey him.

"If you go to that man's induction I'll never forgive you," Louisa concluded.

Mary Isabel said nothing. She just primmed up her lips very determinedly, picked up the silk dress, and carried it to her room.

The next day was fine and warm. Louisa said no word all the morning. She worked fiercely and slammed things around noisily. After dinner Mary Isabel went to her room and came down presently, fine and dainty in her grey silk, with the forget-me-not hat resting on the soft loose waves of her hair. Louisa was blacking the kitchen stove.

She shot one angry glance at Mary Isabel, then gave a short, contemptuous laugh, the laugh of an angry woman who finds herself robbed of all weapons except ridicule.

Mary Isabel flushed and walked with an unfaltering step out of the house and up the lane. She resented Louisa's laughter. She was sure there was nothing so very ridiculous about her appearance. Women far older than she, even in Latimer, wore light dresses and fashionable hats. Really, Louisa was very disagreeable.

"I have put up with her ways too long," thought Mary Isabel, with a quick, unwonted rush of anger. "But I never shall again—no, never, let her be as vexed and scornful as she pleases."

The induction services were interesting, and Mary Isabel enjoyed them. Doctor Hamilton was sitting across from her and once or twice she caught him looking at her admiringly. The doctor noticed the hat and the grey silk and wondered how Mary Isabel had managed to get her own way concerning them. What a pretty woman she was! Really, he had never realized before how very pretty she was. But then, he had never seen her except in a sunbonnet or with her hair combed primly back.

But when the service was over Mary Isabel was dismayed to see that the sky had clouded over and looked very much like rain. Everybody hurried home, and Mary Isabel tripped along the shore road filled with anxious thoughts about her dress. That kind of silk always spotted, and her hat would be ruined if it got wet. How foolish she had been not to bring an umbrella!

She reached her own doorstep panting just as the first drop of rain fell.

"Thank goodness," she breathed.

Then she tried to open the door. It would not open.

She could see Louisa sitting by the kitchen window, calmly reading.

"Louisa, open the door quick," she called impatiently.

Louisa never moved a muscle, although Mary Isabel knew she must have heard.

"Louisa, do you hear what I say?" she cried, reaching

over and tapping on the pane imperiously. "Open the door at once. It is going to rain—it is raining now. Be quick."

Louisa might as well have been a graven image for all the response she gave. Then did Mary Isabel realize her position. Louisa had locked her out purposely, knowing the rain was coming. Louisa had no intention of letting her in; she meant to keep her out until the dress and hat of her rebellion were spoiled. This was Louisa's revenge.

Mary Isabel turned with a gasp. What should she do? The padlocked doors of hen-house and well-house and wood-house: revealed the thoroughness of Louisa's vindictive design. Where should she go? She would go somewhere. She would not have her lovely new dress and hat spoiled!

She caught her ruffled skirts up in her hand and ran across the yard. She climbed the fence into the field and ran across that. Another drop of rain struck her cheek. She never glanced back or she would have seen a horrified face peering from the cottage kitchen window. Louisa had never dreamed that Mary Isabel would seek refuge over at Dr. Hamilton's.

Dr. Hamilton, who had driven home from church with the young minister, saw her coming and ran to open the door for her. Mary Isabel dashed up the verandah steps, breathless, crimson-cheeked, trembling with pent-up indignation and sense of outrage.

"Louisa locked me out, Dr. Hamilton," she cried almost hysterically. "She locked me out on purpose to spoil my dress. I'll never forgive her, I'll never go back to her, never, never, unless she asks me to. I had to come here. I was not going to have my dress ruined to please Louisa."

"Of course not—of course not," said Dr. Hamilton soothingly, drawing her into his big cosy living room. "You did perfectly right to come here, and you are just in time. There is the rain now in good earnest."

Mary Isabel sank into a chair and looked at Dr. Hamilton with tears in her eyes.

"Wasn't it an unkind, unsisterly thing to do?" she asked piteously. "Oh, I shall never feel the same towards Louisa again. Tom was right—I didn't tell you about Tom's letter but I will by and by. I shall not go back to Louisa after her locking me out. When it stops raining I'll go straight up to my cousin Ella's and stay with her until I arrange my plans. But one thing is certain, I shall not go back to Louisa."

"I wouldn't," said the doctor recklessly. "Now, don't cry and don't worry. Take off your hat—you can go to the spare room across the hall, if you like. Jim has gone upstairs to lie down; he has a bad headache and says he doesn't want any tea. So I was going to get up a bachelor's snack for myself. My housekeeper is away. She heard, at church that her mother was ill and went over to Marwood."

When Mary Isabel came back from the spare room, a little calmer but with traces of tears on her pink cheeks, the doctor had as good a tea-table spread as any woman could have had. Mary Isabel thought it was fortunate that the little errand boy, Tommy Brewster, was there, or she certainly would have been dreadfully embarrassed, now that the flame of her anger had blown out. But later on, when tea was over and she and the doctor were left alone, she did not feel embarrassed after all. Instead, she felt delightfully happy and at home. Dr. Hamilton put one so at ease.

She told him all about Tom's letter and her subsequent revolt. Dr. Hamilton never once made the mistake of smiling. He listened and approved and sympathized.

"So I'm determined I won't go back," concluded Mary Isabel, "unless she asks me to—and Louisa will never do that. Ella will be glad enough to have me for a while; she has five children and can't get any help."

The doctor shrugged his shoulders. He thought of Mary Isabel as unofficial drudge to Ella Kemble and her family. Then he looked at the little silvery figure by the window.

"I think I can suggest a better plan," he said gently and tenderly. "Suppose you stay here—as my wife. I've always wanted to ask you that but I feared it was no use because I knew Louisa would oppose it and I did not think you would consent if she did not. I think," the doctor leaned forward and took Mary Isabel's fluttering hand in his, "I think we can be very happy here, dear."

Mary Isabel flushed crimson and her heart beat wildly. She knew now that she loved Dr. Hamilton—and Tom would have liked it—yes, Tom would. She remembered how Tom hated the thought of his sisters being old maids.

"I—think—so—too," she faltered shyly.

"Then," said the doctor briskly, "what is the matter with our being married right here and now?"

"Married!"

"Yes, of course. Here we are in a state where no licence is required, a minister in the house, and you all dressed in the most beautiful wedding silk imaginable. You must see, if you just look at it calmly, how much better it will be than going up to Mrs. Kemble's and thereby publishing your difference with Louisa to all the village. I'll give you fifteen minutes to get used to the idea and then I'll call Jim down."

Mary Isabel put her hands to her face.

"You—you're like a whirlwind," she gasped. "You take away my breath."

"Think it over," said the doctor in a businesslike voice.

Mary Isabel thought—thought very hard for a few moments.

What would Tom have said?

Was it probable that Tom would have approved of such marrying in haste?

Mary Isabel came to the decision that he would have preferred it to having family jars bruited abroad. Moreover, Mary Isabel had never liked Ella Kemble very much. Going to her was only one degree better than going back to Louisa.

At last Mary Isabel took her hands down from her

face. "Well?" said the doctor persuasively as she did so.

"I will consent on one condition," said Mary Isabel firmly. "And that is, that you will let me send word over to Louisa that I am going to be married and that she may come and see the ceremony if she will. Louisa has behaved very unkindly in this matter, but after all she is my sister—and she has been good to me in some ways—and I am not going to give her a chance to say that I got married in this—this headlong-fashion and never let her know."

"Tommy can take the word over," said the doctor.

Mary Isabel went to the doctor's desk and wrote a very brief note.

Dear Louisa:

I am going to be married to Dr. Hamilton right away. I've seen him often at the shore this summer. I would like you to be present at the ceremony if you choose.

Mary Isabel.

Tommy ran across the field with the note.

It had now ceased raining and the clouds were breaking. Mary Isabel thought that a good omen. She and the doctor watched Tommy from the window. They saw Louisa come to the door, take the note, and shut the door in Tommy's face. Ten minutes later she reappeared, habited in her mackintosh, with her second-best bonnet on.

"She's—coming," said Mary Isabel, trembling.

The doctor put his arm protectingly about the little lady.

Mary Isabel tossed her head. "Oh, I'm not—I'm only excited. I shall never be afraid of Louisa again."

Louisa came grimly over the field, up the verandah steps, and into the room without knocking.

"Mary Isabel," she said, glaring at her sister and ignoring the doctor entirely, "did you mean what you said in that letter?"

"Yes, I did," said Mary Isabel firmly.

"You are going to be married to that man in this shameless, indecent haste?"

"Yes."

"And nothing I can say will have the least effect on you?"

"Not the slightest."

"Then," said Louisa, more grimly than ever, "all I ask of you is to come home and be married from under your father's roof. Do have that much respect for your parents' memory, at least."

"Of course I will," cried Mary Isabel impulsively, softening at once. "Of course we will—won't we?" she asked, turning prettily to the doctor.

"Just as you say," he answered gallantly.

Louisa snorted. "I'll go home and air the parlour," she said. "It's lucky I baked that fruitcake Monday. You can come when you're ready."

She stalked home across the field. In a few minutes the doctor and Mary Isabel followed, and behind them came the young minister, carrying his blue book under his arm, and trying hard and not altogether successfully to look grave.

Aunt Philippa and the Men

I knew quite well why Father sent me to Prince Edward Island to visit Aunt Philippa that summer. He told me he was sending me there "to learn some sense"; and my stepmother, of whom I was very fond, told me she was sure the sea air would do me a world of good. I did not want to learn sense or be done a world of good; I wanted to stay in Montreal and go on being foolish—and make up my quarrel with Mark Fenwick. Father and Mother did not know anything about this quarrel; they thought I was still on good terms with him—and that is why they sent me to Prince Edward Island.

I was very miserable. I did not want to go to Aunt Philippa's. It was not because I feared it would be dull—for without Mark, Montreal was just as much of a howling wilderness as any other place. But it was so horribly far away. When the time came for Mark to want to make up—as come I knew it would—how could he do it if I were seven hundred miles away?

Nevertheless, I went to Prince Edward Island. In all my eighteen years I had never once disobeyed Father. He is a very hard man to disobey. I knew I should have to make a beginning some time if I wanted to marry Mark, so I saved all my little courage up for that and didn't waste any of it opposing the visit to Aunt Philippa.

I couldn't understand Father's point of view. Of course, he hated old John Fenwick, who had once sued him for libel and won the case. Father had written an indiscreet editorial in the excitement of a red-hot political contest—and was made to understand that there are some things you can't say of another man even at election time. But then, he need not have hated Mark because of that; Mark was not even born when it happened.

Old John Fenwick was not much better pleased about Mark and me than Father was, though he didn't go to the length of forbidding it; he just acted grumpily and disagreeably. Things were unpleasant enough all round without a quarrel between Mark and me; yet quarrel we did—and over next to nothing, too, you understand. And now I had to set out for Prince Edward Island without even seeing him, for he was away in Toronto on business.

* * *

When my train reached Copely the next afternoon, Aunt Philippa was waiting for me. There was nobody else in sight, but I would have known her had there been a thousand. Nobody but Aunt Philippa could have that determined mouth, those piercing grey eyes, and that pronounced, unmistakable Goodwin nose. And certainly nobody but Aunt Philippa would have come to meet me arrayed in a wrapper of chocolate print with huge yellow roses scattered over it, and a striped blue-and-white apron!

She welcomed me kindly but absent-mindedly, her thoughts evidently being concentrated on the problem of getting my trunk home. I had only the one, and in Montreal it had seemed to be of moderate size; but on the platform of Copely station, sized up by Aunt Philippa's merciless eye, it certainly looked huge.

"I thought we could a-took it along tied on the back of the buggy," she said disapprovingly, "but I guess we'll have to leave it, and I'll send the hired boy over for it tonight. You can get along without it till then, I s'pose?"

There was a fine irony in her tone. I hastened to assure her meekly that I could, and that it did not matter if my trunk could not be taken up till next day.

"Oh, Jerry can come for it tonight as well as not," said

Aunt Philippa, as we climbed into her buggy. "I'd a good notion to send him to meet you, for he isn't doing much today, and I wanted to go to Mrs. Roderick MacAllister's funeral. But my head was aching me so bad I thought I wouldn't enjoy the funeral if I did go. My head is better now, so I kind of wish I had gone. She was a hundred and four years old and I'd always promised myself that I'd go to her funeral."

Aunt Philippa's tone was melancholy. She did not recover her good spirits until we were out on the pretty, grassy, elm-shaded country road, garlanded with its ribbon of buttercups. Then she suddenly turned around and looked me over scrutinizingly.

"You're not as good-looking as I expected from your picture, but them photographs always flatter. That's the reason I never had any took. You're rather thin and brown. But you've good eyes and you look clever. Your father writ me you hadn't much sense, though. He wants me to teach you some, but it's a thankless business. People would rather be fools."

Aunt Philippa struck her steed smartly with the whip and controlled his resultant friskiness with admirable skill.

"Well, you know it's pleasanter," I said, wickedly. "Just think what a doleful world it would be if everybody were sensible."

Aunt Philippa looked at me out of the corner of her eye and disdained any skirmish of flippant epigram.

"So you want to get married?" she said. "You'd better wait till you're grown up."

"How old must a person be before she is grown up?" I asked gravely.

"Humph! That depends. Some are grown up when they're born, and others ain't grown up when they're eighty. That same Mrs. Roderick I was speaking of never grew up. She was as foolish when she was a hundred as when she was ten."

"Perhaps that's why she lived so long," I suggested. All thought of seeking sympathy in Aunt Philippa had vanished. I resolved I would not even mention Mark's name.

"Mebbe 'twas," admitted Aunt Philippa with a grim smile. "*I'd* rather live fifty sensible years than a hundred foolish ones."

Much to my relief, she made no further reference to my affairs. As we rounded a curve in the road where two great over-arching elms met, a buggy wheeled by us, occupied by a young man in clerical costume. He had a pleasant boyish face, and he touched his hat courteously. Aunt Philippa nodded very frostily and gave her horse a quite undeserved cut.

"There's a man you don't want to have much to do with," she said portentously. "He's a Methodist minister."

"Why, Auntie, the Methodists are a very nice denomination," I protested. "My stepmother is a Methodist, you know."

"No, I didn't know, but I'd believe anything of a stepmother. I've no use for Methodists or their ministers. This fellow just came last spring, and it's *my* opinion he smokes. And he thinks every girl who looks at him falls in love with him—as if a Methodist minister was any prize! Don't you take much notice of him, Ursula."

"I'll not be likely to have the chance," I said, with an amused smile.

"Oh, you'll see enough of him. He boards at Mrs. John Callman's, just across the road from us, and he's always out sunning himself on her verandah. Never studies, of course. Last Sunday they say he preached on the iron that floated. If he'd confine himself to the Bible and leave sensational subjects alone it would be better for him and his poor congregation, and so I told Mrs. John Callman to her face. I should think *she* would have had enough of his sex by this time. She married John Callman against her father's will, and he had delirious trembles for years. That's the men for you."

"They're not *all* like that, Aunt Philippa," I protested.

"Most of 'em are. See that house over there? Mrs. Jane Harrison lives there. Her husband took tantrums every few days or so and wouldn't get out of bed. She had to do all the barn work till he'd got over his spell. That's men for you. When he died, people writ her letters of condolence but *I* just sot down and writ her one of congratulation. There's the Presbyterian manse in the hollow. Mr. Bentwell's our minister. He's a good man and he'd be a rather nice one if he didn't think it was his duty to be a little miserable all the time. He won't let his wife wear a fashionable hat, and his daughter can't fix her hair the way she wants to. Even being a minister can't prevent a man from being a crank. Here's Ebenezer Milgrave coming. You take a good look at him. He used to be insane for years. He believed he was dead and used to rage at his wife because she wouldn't bury him. *I'd* a-done it."

Aunt Philippa looked so determinedly grim that I could almost see her with a spade in her hand. I laughed aloud at the picture summoned up.

"Yes, it's funny, but I guess his poor wife didn't find it very humorsome. He's been pretty sane for some years now, but you never can tell when he'll break out again. He's got a brother, Albert Milgrave, who's been married twice. They say he was courting his second wife while his first was dying. Let that be as it may, he used his first wife's wedding ring to marry the second. That's the men for you."

"Don't you know *any* good husbands, Aunt Philippa?" I asked desperately.

"Oh, yes, lots of 'em—over there," said Aunt Philippa sardonically, waving her whip in the direction of a little country graveyard on a distant hill.

"Yes, but *living*—walking about in the flesh?"

"Precious few. Now and again you'll come across a man whose wife won't put up with any nonsense and he *has* to be respectable. But the most of 'em are poor bargains—poor bargains."

"And are all the wives saints?" I persisted.

"Laws, no, but they're too good for the men," retorted Aunt Philippa, as she turned in at her own gate. Her house was close to the road and was painted such a vivid green that the landscape looked faded by contrast. Across the gable end of it was the legend, "Philippa's Farm," emblazoned in huge black letters two feet long. All its surroundings were very neat. On the kitchen doorstep a patchwork cat was making a grave toilet. The groundwork of the cat was white, and its spots were black, yellow, grey, and brown.

"There's Joseph," said Aunt Philippa. "I call him that because his coat is of many colours. But I ain't no lover of cats. They're too much like the men to suit me."

"Cats have always been supposed to be peculiarly feminine," I said, descending.

"'Twas a man that supposed it, then," retorted Aunt Philippa, beckoning to her hired boy. "Here, Jerry, put Prince away. Jerry's a good sort of boy," she confided to me as we went into the house. "I had Jim Spencer last summer and the only good thing about *him* was his appetite. I put up with him till harvest was in, and then one day my patience give out. He upsot a churnful of cream in the back yard—and was just as cool as a cowcumber over it—laughed and said it was good for the land. I told him I wasn't in the habit of fertilizing my back yard with cream. But that's the men for you. Come in. I'll have tea ready in no time. I sot the table before I left. There's lemon pie. Mrs. John Cantwell sent it over. I never make lemon pie myself. Ten years ago I took the prize for lemon pies at the county fair, and I've never made any since for fear I'd lose my reputation for them."

*   *   *

The first month of my stay passed not unpleasantly. The summer weather was delightful, and the sea air was certainly splendid. Aunt Philippa's little farm ran right down to the shore, and I spent much of my time there. There were also several families of cousins to be visited in the farmhouses that dotted the pretty, seaward-sloping valley, and they came back to see me at

173

"Philippa's Farm." I picked spruce gum and berries and ferns, and Aunt Philippa taught me to make butter. It was all very idyllic—or would have been if Mark had written. But Mark did not write. I supposed he must be very angry because I had run off to Prince Edward Island without so much as a note of goodbye. But I had been so sure he would understand!

Aunt Philippa never made any further reference to the reason Father had sent me to her, but she allowed no day to pass without holding up to me some horrible example of matrimonial infelicity. The number of unhappy wives who walked or drove past "Philippa's Farm" every afternoon, as we sat on the verandah, was truly pitiable.

We always sat on the verandah in the afternoon, when we were not visiting or being visited. I made a pretence of fancy work, and Aunt Philippa spun diligently on a little old-fashioned spinning-wheel that had been her grandmother's. She always sat before the wood stand which held her flowers, and the gorgeous blots of geranium blossom and big green leaves furnished a pretty background. She always wore her shapeless but clean print wrappers, and her iron-grey hair was always combed neatly down over her ears. Joseph sat between us, sleeping or purring. She spun so expertly that she could keep a close watch on the road as well, and I got the biography of every individual who went by. As for the poor young Methodist minister, who liked to read or walk on the verandah of our neighbour's house, Aunt Philippa never had a good word for him. I had met him once or twice socially and had liked him. I wanted to ask him to call but dared not—Aunt Philippa had vowed he should never enter her house.

"If I was dead and he came to my funeral I'd rise up and order him out," she said.

"I thought he made a very nice prayer at Mrs. Seaman's funeral the other day," I said.

"Oh, I've no doubt he can pray. I never heard anyone make more beautiful prayers than old Simon Kennedy down at the harbour, who was always drunk or hoping to be—and the drunker he was the better he prayed. It ain't no matter how well a man prays if his preaching isn't right. That Methodist man preaches a lot of things that ain't true, and what's worse they ain't sound doctrine. At least, that's what I've heard. I never was in a Methodist church, thank goodness."

"Don't you think Methodists go to heaven as well as Presbyterians, Aunt Philippa?" I asked gravely.

"That ain't for us to decide," said Aunt Philippa solemnly. "It's in higher hands than ours. But I ain't going to associate with them on *earth*, whatever I may have to do in heaven. The folks round here mostly don't make much difference and go to the Methodist church quite often. But *I* say if you are a Presbyterian, *be* a Presbyterian. Of course, if you ain't, it don't matter much what you do. As for that minister man, he has a grand-uncle who was sent to the penitentiary for embezzlement. I found out *that* much."

And evidently Aunt Philippa had taken an unholy joy in finding it out.

"I dare say some of our own ancestors deserved to go to the penitentiary, even if they never did," I remarked. "Who is that woman driving past, Aunt Philippa? She must have been very pretty once."

"She was—and that was all the good it did her. 'Favour is deceitful and beauty is vain,' Ursula. She was Sarah Pyatt and she married Fred Proctor. He was one of your wicked, fascinating men. After she married him he give up being fascinating but he kept on being wicked. *That's* the men for you. Her sister Flora weren't much luckier. *Her* man was that domineering she couldn't call her soul her own. Finally he couldn't get his own way over something and he just suicided by jumping into the well. A good riddance—but of course the well was spoiled. Flora could never abide the thought of using it again, poor thing. *That's* men for you.

"And there's that old Enoch Allan on his way to the station. He's ninety if he's a day. You can't kill some folks with a meat axe. His wife died twenty years ago. He'd been married when he was twenty so they'd lived together for fifty years. She was a faithful, hard-working creature and kept him out of the poorhouse, for he was a shiftless soul, not lazy, exactly, but just too fond of sitting. But he weren't grateful. She had a kind of bitter tongue and they did use to fight scandalous. O' course it was all his fault. Well, she died, and old Enoch and my father drove together to the graveyard. Old Enoch was awful quiet all the way there and back, but just afore they got home, he says solemnly to Father: 'You mayn't believe it, Henry, but this is the happiest day of my life.' *That's* men for you. His brother, Scotty Allan, was the meanest man ever lived in these parts. When his wife died she was buried with a little gold brooch in her collar unbeknownst to him. When he found it out he went one night to the graveyard and opened up the grave and the casket to get that brooch."

"Oh, Aunt Philippa, that is a horrible story," I cried, recoiling with a shiver over the gruesomeness of it.

"'Course it is, but what would you expect of a man?" retorted Aunt Philippa.

Somehow, her stories began to affect me in spite of myself. There were times when I felt very dreary. Perhaps Aunt Philippa was right. Perhaps men possessed neither truth nor constancy. Certainly Mark had forgotten me. I was ashamed of myself because this hurt me so much, but I could not help it. I grew pale and listless. Aunt Philippa sometimes peered at me sharply, but she held her peace. I was grateful for this.

* * *

But one day a letter did come from Mark. I dared not read it until I was safely in my own room. Then I opened it with trembling fingers.

The letter was a little stiff. Evidently Mark was feeling sore enough over things. He made no reference to our quarrel or to my sojourn in Prince Edward Island. He wrote that his firm was sending him to South Africa to take charge of their interests there. He would leave in three weeks' time and could not return for five years. If I still cared anything for him, would I meet him in Halifax, marry him, and go to South Africa with him? If I would not, he would understand that I had ceased to love him and that all was over between us.

That, boiled down, was the gist of Mark's letter. When I had read it I cast myself on the bed and wept out all the tears I had refused to let myself shed during my weeks of exile.

For I could not do what Mark asked—I *could not*. I couldn't run away to be married in that desolate, unbefriended fashion. It would be a disgrace. I would feel ashamed of it all my life and be unhappy over it. I thought that Mark was rather unreasonable. He knew what my feelings about run-away marriages were. And was it absolutely necessary for him to go to South Africa? Of course his father was behind it somewhere, but surely he could have got out of it if he had really tried.

Well, if he went to South Africa he must go alone. But my heart would break.

I cried the whole afternoon, cowering among my pillows. I never wanted to go out of that room again. I never wanted to see anybody again. I hated the thought of facing Aunt Philippa with her cold eyes and her miserable stories that seemed to strip life of all beauty and love of all reality. I could hear her scornful, "That's the men for you," if she heard what was in Mark's letter.

"What is the matter, Ursula?"

Aunt Philippa was standing by my bed. I was too abject to resent her coming in without knocking.

"Nothing," I said spiritlessly.

"If you've been crying for three mortal hours over nothing you want a good spanking and you'll get it," observed Aunt Philippa placidly, sitting down on my trunk. "Get right up off that bed this minute and tell me what the trouble is. I'm bound to know, for I'm in your father's place at present."

"There, then!" I flung her Mark's letter. There wasn't

anything in it that it was sacrilege to let another person see. That was one reason why I had been crying.

Aunt Philippa read it over twice. Then she folded it up deliberately and put it back in the envelope.

"What are you going to do?" she asked in a matter-of-fact tone.

"I'm not going to run away to be married," I answered sullenly.

"Well, no, I wouldn't advise you to," said Aunt Philippa reflectively. "It's a kind of low-down thing to do, though there's been a terrible lot of romantic nonsense talked and writ about eloping. It may be a painful necessity sometimes, but it ain't in this case. You write to your young man and tell him to come here and be married respectable under my roof, same as a Goodwin ought to."

I sat up and stared at Aunt Philippa. I was so amazed that it is useless to try to express my amazement.

"Aunt—Philippa," I gasped. "I thought—I thought—"

"You thought I was a hard old customer, and so I am," said Aunt Philippa. "But I don't take my opinions from your father nor anybody else. It didn't prejudice me any against your young man that your father didn't like him. I knew your father of old. I have some other friends in Montreal and I writ to them and asked them what he was like. From what they said I judged he was decent enough as men go. You're too young to be married, but if you let him go off to South Africa he'll slip through your fingers for sure, and I s'pose you're like some of the rest of us—nobody'll do you but the one. So tell him to come here and be married."

"I don't see how I can," I gasped. "I can't get ready to be married in three weeks. I can't—"

"I should think you have enough clothes in that trunk to do you for a spell," said Aunt Philippa sarcastically. "You've more than my mother ever had in all her life. We'll get you a wedding dress of some kind. You can get it made in Charlottetown, if country dressmakers aren't good enough for you, and I'll bake you a wedding cake that'll taste as good as anything you could get in Montreal, even if it won't look so stylish."

"What will Father say?" I questioned.

"Lots o' things," conceded Aunt Philippa grimly. "But I don't see as it matters when neither you nor me'll be there to have our feelings hurt. I'll write a few things to your father. He hasn't got much sense. He ought to be thankful to get a decent young man for his son-in-law in a world where most every man is a wolf in sheep's clothing. But that's the men for you."

And that was Aunt Philippa for you. For the next three weeks she was a blissfully excited, busy woman. I was allowed to choose the material and fashion of my wedding suit and hat myself, but almost everything else was settled by Aunt Philippa. I didn't mind; it was a relief to be rid of all responsibility; I did protest when she declared her intention of having a big wedding and asking all the cousins and semi-cousins on the island, but Aunt Philippa swept my objections lightly aside.

"I'm bound to have one good wedding in this house," she said. "Not likely I'll ever have another chance."

She found time amid all the baking and concocting to warn me frequently not to take it too much to heart if Mark failed to come after all.

"I know a man who jilted a girl on her wedding day. That's the men for you. It's best to be prepared."

But Mark did come, getting there the evening before our wedding day. And then a severe blow fell on Aunt Philippa. Word came from the manse that Mr. Bentwell had been suddenly summoned to Nova Scotia to his mother's deathbed; he had started that night.

"That's the men for you," said Aunt Philippa bitterly. "Never can depend on one of them, not even on a minister. What's to be done now?"

"Get another minister," said Mark easily.

"Where'll you get him?" demanded Aunt Philippa. "The minister at Cliftonville is away on his vacation, and Mercer is vacant, and that leaves none nearer than town. It won't do to depend on a town minister being able to come. No, there's no help for it. You'll have to have that Methodist man."

Aunt Philippa's tone was tragic. Plainly she thought the ceremony would scarcely be legal if that Methodist man married us. But neither Mark nor I cared. We were too happy to be disturbed by any such trifles.

The young Methodist minister married us the next day in the presence of many beaming guests. Aunt Philippa, splendid in black silk and point-lace collar, neither of which lost a whit of dignity or lustre by being made ten years before, was composure itself while the ceremony was going on. But no sooner had the minister pronounced us man and wife than she spoke up.

"Now that's over I want someone to go right out and put out the fire on the kitchen roof. It's been on fire for the last ten minutes."

Minister and bridegroom headed the emergency brigade, and Aunt Philippa pumped the water for them. In a short time the fire was out, all was safe, and we were receiving our deferred congratulations.

"Now, young man," said Aunt Philippa solemnly as she shook hands with Mark, "don't you ever try to get out of this, even if a Methodist minister did marry you."

She insisted on driving us to the train and said goodbye to us as we stood on the car steps. She had caught more of the shower of rice than I had, and as the day was hot and sunny she had tied over her head, atop of that festal silk dress, a huge, home-made, untrimmed straw hat. But she did not look ridiculous. There was a certain dignity about Aunt Philippa in any costume and under any circumstance.

"Aunt Philippa," I said, "tell me this: why have you helped me to be married?"

The train began to move.

"I refused once to run away myself, and I've repented it ever since." Then, as the train gathered speed and the distance between us widened, she shouted after us, "But I s'pose if I had run away I'd have repented of that too."

A Girl's Place at Dalhousie College

Essay first published in *The Halifax Herald*, 1896.

"Why, sirs, they do all this as well as we."

"Girls,
Knowledge is now no more a fountain sealed;
  Drink deep until the habits of the slave,
The sins of emptiness, gossip and spite,
  And slander, die. Better not be at all
Than not be noble."

"Pretty were the sight,
If our old halls could change their sex and flaunt
  With prudes for proctors, dowagers for deans,
And sweet girl graduates in their golden hair."

Tennyson—"The Princess."

It is not a very long time, as time goes in the world's history, since the idea of educating a girl beyond her "three r's" would have been greeted with up lifted hands and shocked countenances. What! Could any girl, in her right and proper senses, ask for any higher, more advanced education than that accorded her by tradition and custom? Could any girl presume to think that the attainments of her mother and grandmother before her, insufficient for her? Above all, could the dream of opposing her weak feminine mind to the mighty masculine intellect which had been dominating the world of knowledge from a date long preceding the time when Hypatia was torn to pieces by a mob of Alexandria?

"Never," was the approved answer to all such questions. Girls were "educated" according to the standard of the time. That is they were taught reading and writing and a small smattering of foreign languages; they "took" music and were trained to warble pretty little songs and instructed in the mysteries of embroidery and drawing. The larger proportion of them, of course, married, and we are quite ready to admit that they made none the poorer wives and mothers because they could not conjugate a Greek verb or demonstrate a proposition in Euclid. It is not the purpose of this article to discuss whether, with a broader education, they might not have fulfilled the duties of wifehood and motherhood equally well and with much more of ease to themselves and others.

Old traditions die hard and we will step very gently around their death bed. But there was always a certain number of unfortunates—let us call them so since the world would persist in using the term—who, for no fault of their own probably, were left to braid St. Catherine's tresses for the term of their natural lives; and a hard lot truly was theirs in the past. If they did not live in meek dependence with some compassionate relative, eating the bitter bread of unappreciated drudgery, it was because they could earn a meagre and precarious subsistance in the few and underpaid occupations then open to women. They could do nothing else! Their education had not fitted them to cope with any and every destiny; they were helpless straws, swept along the merciless current of existence.

If some woman, with the courage of her convictions, dared to make a stand against the popular prejudice, she was sneered at as a "blue-stocking," and prudent mothers held her up as a warning example to their pretty, frivolous daughters, and looked askance at her as a not altogether desirable curiosity.

But, nowadays, all this is so changed that we are inclined to wonder if it has not taken longer than a generation to effect the change. The "higher education of women" has passed into a common place phrase.

A girl is no longer shut out from the temple of knowledge simply because she is a girl; she can compete, and has competed, successfully with her brother in all his classes. The way is made easy before her feet; there is no struggle to render her less sweet and womanly, and the society of to-day is proud of its "sweet girl-graduates."

If they marry, their husbands find in their wives an increased capacity for assistance and sympathy; their children can look up to their mothers for the clear-cut judgment and the wisest guidance. If they do not marry, their lives are still full and happy and useful; they have something to do and can do it well, and the world is better off from their having been born in it.

In England there have been two particularly brilliant examples of what a girl can do when she is given an equal chance with her brother; these are so widely known that it is hardly necessary to name them. Every one has read and heard of Miss Fawcett, the brilliant mathematician, who came out ahead of the senior wrangles at Cambridge, and of Miss Ramsay, who led the classical tripos at the same university.

In the new world, too, many girl students have made for themselves a brilliant record. Here, every opportunity and aid is offered to the girl who longs for the best education the age can yield her. There are splendidly equipped colleges for women, equal in every respect to those for men; or, if a girl prefers co-education and wishes to match her intellect with man's on a common footing, the doors of many universities are open to her. Canada is well to the front in this respect and Dalhousie college, Halifax, claims, I believe, to have been the second college in the Dominion to admit girl students, if we can use the word "admit" of an institution which was never barred to them. Girls, had they so elected, might have paced, with notebook and lexicon, Dalhousie's classic halls from the time of its founding. When the first application for the admission of a girl to the college was received, the powers that were met together in solemn conclave to deliberate thereon, and it was found that there was nothing in the charter of the college to prevent the admission of a girl.

Accordingly, in 1881 two girls, Miss Newcombe and Miss Calkin, were enrolled as students at Dalhousie. Miss Calkin did not complete her course, but Miss Newcombe did and graduated in 1885 with honors in English and English history,—the first of a goodly number who have followed in her footsteps. Miss Newcombe afterwards became Mrs. Trusman and is now on the staff of the Halifax Ladies' college. In 1882 Miss Stewart entered, took the science course and graduated in 1886 as B.Sc. with honors in mathematics and mathematical physics.

In 1887 three girls graduated, Miss Forbes and Miss MacNeill each took their degree of B.A., the latter with high honors in English and English history. The third, Miss Ritchie, the most brilliant of Dalhousie's girl graduates took her B.L., she then took her Ph.D., at Cornell university and is now associate professor of philosophy in Wellesley college. Then occurs a hiatus in the list, for we find no girls graduating till 1891 when there were four who received their degrees, Miss Goodwin, Miss McNaughton and Miss Baxter in arts; Miss Muir took her degree of B.L.

In 1892 Miss Baxter, who had graduated with high honors in mathematics and mathematical physics, took her degree of M.A., after which she went to Cornell and there gained a Ph.D.

Miss Muir took her M.L., in 1893 and has since been studying for a Ph.D., at Cornell. In 1892 three girls, Miss Weston, Miss Archibald and Miss Harrington, obtained their B.A. degree. Miss Archibald graduated with great distinction and took her M.A. in 1891. Afterwards she went to Bryn Mawr college, winning a scholarship at her entrance. Miss Harrington graduated with high honors in

English and English literature and became M.A. in 1894. She also won a scholarship at Bryn Mawr, where she is at present studying.

In 1893 the two girl graduates were Miss McDonald and Miss Murray, the latter of whom took high honors in philosophy and is now on the staff of the Ladies college. The graduates of 1894 were Miss Hebb, B.A., Miss Hobrecker, B.A., Miss Jameison, B.A., and Miss Ross, B.A. Miss Hobrecker took honors in English and German. Miss Jameison and Miss McKenzie each took their M.A. in 1895. Miss Ross graduated with high honors in mathematics and mathematical physics. In 1895 three girls graduated B.A. Miss McDonald took honors in mathematics and mathematical physics; Miss Ross was the second Dalhousie girl to graduate with "great distinction," and takes her M.A. this year. Miss Bent is at present studying for her M.A.

It will be seen, from those statements, that, out of the twenty-five girls who have graduated from Dalhousie, nearly all have done remarkably well in their studies, and attained to striking success in their examinations. This, in itself, testifies to their ability to compete with masculine minds on a common level. This year there is a larger number of girls in attendance at Dalhousie than there has been in any previous year. In all, there are about fifty-eight, including the lady medical students. Of course, out of these fifty-eight a large proportion are not undergraduates. They are merely general students taking classes in some favorite subject, usually languages and history.

In all, there are about twenty-nine undergraduate girls in attendance this session. The number of girls in the freshman class is the largest that has yet been seen at Dalhousie. Out of the twenty-six girls, at whom disdainful sophs are privileged to hurl all the old jokes that have been dedicated to freshmen since time immemorial, there are nine undergraduates. In the second year are eleven girls, eight of whom are undergraduates; and in the third year six out of the nine girls are also undergraduates.

There are also nine girls in the fourth year, seven of whom graduate this session. This is the largest class of girls which has yet graduated from Dalhousie. Several of these are taking honors and will, it is expected, amply sustain the reputation which girl students have won for themselves at the university. No girl has as yet attempted to take a full course in law at Dalhousie. Not that any one doubts or disputes the ability of a girl to master the mysteries of "contracts" or even the intricacies of "equity jurisprudence;" but the Barristers' act, we believe, stands ruthlessly in the way of any enterprising maiden who might wish to choose law for a profession.

However, we did hear a different reason advanced not long ago by one who had thought the subject over. He was a lawyer himself, by the way, so no one need bring an action against us for libel. "Oh, girls," he said, "Girls were never cut out for lawyers. They've got too much conscience." We have been trying ever since to find out if he were speaking sarcastically or in good faith.

But, if shut out from the bar, they are admitted to the study and practise of medicine and two girls have graduated from the Halifax medical college as full fledged M.D.'s. One of these, Miss Hamilton, obtained her degree in 1894 and has since been practising in Halifax. In 1895 Miss McKay graduated and is now, we understand, practising in New Glasgow. There are at present three girl students at the medical college. One will graduate this year; of the other two, one is in the third, and one in the first year.

———————

Dalhousie is strictly co-educational. The girls enter on exactly the same footing as the men and are admitted to an equal share in all the privileges of the institution. The only places from which they are barred are the gymnasium and reading room. They are really excluded from the former, but there is nothing to keep them out of the reading room save custom and tradition. It is the domain sacred to masculine scrimmages and gossips and the girls religiously avoid it, never doing more than cast speculative glances at its door as they scurry past into the library. We have not been able to discover what the penalty would be if a girl should venture into the reading room. It may be death or it may be only banishment for life.

The library, however is free to all. The girls can prowl around there in peace, bury themselves in encyclopedias, pore over biographies and exercise their wits on logic, or else they can get into a group and carry on whispered discussions which may have reference to their work or may not.

They take prominent part in some of the college societies. In the Y.M.C.A. their assistance is limited to preparing papers on subjects connected with missions and reading them on the public nights; in the Philomathic society they are more actively engaged. The object of this society is to stimulate interest and inquiry in literature, science and philosophy. Girls are elected on the executive committee and papers on literary subjects are prepared and read by them throughout the session.

They are also initiated into the rites and ceremonies of the philosophical club and are very much in demand in the Glee club. Once in a while, too, a girl is found on the editorial staff of the Dalhousie Gazette, and what the jokes column would do, if stripped of allusions to them, is beyond our comprehension.

The athletic club, however, numbers no girls among its devotees and it does not seem probable that it will—certainly not in this generation, at least. The question of the higher education of girls involves a great many interesting problems which are frequently discussed but which time alone can solve satisfactorily. Woman has asserted her claim to an equal educational standing with man and that claim has been conceded to her. What use then, will she make of her privileges? Will she take full advantage of them or will she merely play with them until, tired of the novelty, she drops them for some mere fad? Every year since girls first entered Dalhousie, has witnessed a steady increase in the number of them in attendance; and it is to be expected that, in the years to come, the number will be very much larger. But beyond a certain point we do not think it will go. It is not likely that the day will ever come when the number of girl students at Dalhousie, or at any other co-educational university, will be equal to the number of men. There will always be a certain number of clever ambitious girls who, feeling that their best life work can be accomplished only when backed up by a broad and thorough education, will take a university course, will work conscientiously and earnestly and will share all the honors and successes of their brothers. There will, however, always be a limit to the number of such girls.

Again, we have frequently heard this question asked: "Is it, in the end, worth while for a girl to take a university course with all its attendant expense, hard work, and risk of health?" How many girls, out of those who graduate from the universities, are ever heard of prominently again, many of them marrying or teaching school? Would not an ordinarily good education have benefited them quite as much? Is it then worth while, from this standpoint, for any girl who is not exceptionally brilliant, to take a university course?

The individual question of "worth while" or "not worth while" is one which every girl must scramble for herself. It is only in its general aspect that we must look at the subject. In the first place, as far as distinguishing themselves in after life goes, take the number of girls who have graduated from Dalhousie—say thirty, most of whom are yet in their twenties and have their whole lives before them. Out of that thirty, eight or nine at the very least have not stood still but have gone forward successfully and are known to the public as brilliant, efficient workers. Out of any thirty men who graduate, how many in the same time do better or even as well? This, however, is looking at the question from the standpoint that the main object of a girl in taking a university course is to keep herself before the public as a distinguished worker. But is it? No! At least it should not be. Such an ambition is not the end and aim of a true education.

A girl does not—or, at least, should not—go to a university merely to shine as clever students take honors, "get through and then do something very brilliant." Nay; she goes—or should go—to prepare herself for living, not alone in the finite but in the infinite. She goes to have her mind broadened and her powers of observation cultivated. She goes to study her own race in all the bewildering perplexities of its being. In short, she goes to find out the best, easiest and most effective way of living the life that God and nature planned out for her to live.

If a girl gets this out of her college course, it is of little consequence whether her after "career" be brilliant, as the world defines brilliancy, or not. She has obtained that from her studies which will stand by her all her life, and future generations will rise up and call her blessed, who handed down to them the clear insight, the broad sympathy with their fellow creatures, the energy of purpose and the self-control that such a woman must transmit to those who come after her.